MW01178927

Wave Watch

Lesley Choyce

Formac Publishing Limited
Halifax, Nova Scotia

Cover illustration: Mike Little

Canadian Cataloguing in Publication
Choyce, Lesley, 1951 -
    ISBN 0-88780-080-7 (pbk.)
    ISBN 0-88780-081-5 (bound)
I. Title.
PS8555.H69W38 1990 jC813'.54   C90-097659-4
PZ7.C46Ws 1990

Formac Publishing Company Limited
5502 Atlantic Street,
Halifax, N.S. B3H 1G4

Printed and bound in Canada

Chapter One

The Critical Zone

It was my birthday. Finally I was sixteen. I had just kissed goodbye forever to being fifteen years old. And here I was, sitting on my surfboard off Lawrencetown headland watching the sun pull itself up out of the Atlantic Ocean. It was just this big red ball of light that seemed to send a trail of fire right straight at me across the water.

My mom said I should have a big breakfast before going out surfing, but I said, forget it. I wanted to be in the water when the sun came up. And my old man — he told me it was too cold to be in the water.

"It's only April, Randy. Heck, boy, we raised you to have more sense than this," he said. "It's not even summer yet. Shoot, it doesn't hardly feel like winter's done with us."

"The wetsuit keeps me warm," I reminded him.

"Nothing could keep me warm out there. Nothing. You wouldn't catch me out in some god-forsaken ocean first thing on a cold morning. I'd rather you just cover me over with ice and leave me there." Then he put on his old coveralls and headed out to the welding shop behind our house where he'd work straight through until my mother called him for lunch.

Kevin, my big brother, was a little more helpful. "C'mon, Rankle, I'll give you a ride." Randy is my real name, but a few people still call me by my nickname from when I was a kid. Kevin was headed off to go fishing. His boat was tied up at the wharf on Causeway Road. All the other men would be well to sea by now. Kev was late as usual.

It had been a cold winter. There was still some slush ice in the water. Nothing serious, just the junk that washes out of the river from the lake. I'll tell you the truth: I was glad to be away from my family. I was right happy to be completely alone, on my old board, trying to wiggle my toes back and forth inside my wetsuit boots to warm them up. All I needed was the right wave.

Then I saw it. There was a set headed towards me. Looked like five decent swells. The fifth was the biggest — not huge, mind you — but it would be a solid six-foot wall by the time it made it to me.

Just then something happened that made my heart stop. Something popped up right alongside of me, not three feet from my board. At first I thought it must be a shark. I'm scared stiff that some day a shark will come up out of nowhere and chew my foot right off. I've never even seen a shark up close, but the thought of pulling a bloody stump of a leg out of the water after a shark has had my foot for breakfast — well, that just scares the living daylights out of me.

But it was no shark. It was a seal ... not even a big momma like some of them I've seen that are six or seven hundred pounds. This was just a young one. He had beautiful eyes and he looked right at me. He wasn't scared at all. I swallowed hard to calm myself down. I felt the first few waves pass under me and got a little tense with anticipation. Then I found my wave. This was the one, I knew, as I started paddling on my belly. This is the first wave of the rest of my life, I thought, wondering where did I get such weird stuff in my head. But that's what it felt like. I was sixteen years old. I'd have my learner's permit today, and in six weeks, my for real license. My life was just about to begin.

I let out a big wild whoop, loud enough to be heard halfway down the Eastern Shore. I felt the speed of the wave now catch onto me. My yell scared the seal pup, and he slipped under just as I took off.

Then it was just like automatic pilot. In a single, perfect fluid motion, I was grabbing the rails of my board and pushing myself onto my feet. The wave was just hitting the shallows near the headland. I could feel all that power building behind me. I could hear the sound of the slush ice against my board, like someone crumbling up aluminum foil.

I knew that this was the new me, the one in control, the one who could tap the power. Not the kid at school, the klutz, the chubby, goofy Randy who clunked through life.

No, man, this was it. I dropped to the bottom of the face of the wave, jammed a bottom turn and kicked back high up into the face of it. Behind me now it was starting to break. I was on a smooth slide across a long, beautiful wave that reached from the headland way down the beach. But I was already way out on the shoulder. This was too easy. I carved a turn off the top and cranked back into the wave. Go for the danger, said the voice inside me.

I went for it. I drove straight into the collapsing wall and punched right up through the white water until I could make a floater right down to the bottom again. Then I was back up onto the clean, even-breaking wall and cruising down the line.

The wave was starting to tube and I let myself slip back into the critical zone again. My back was to the wall. I couldn't see for sure how close to the crunch I was. I didn't care. I'd take my chances. I crouched low, just in time to see the wave leap out over my head.

It was such a clean, crisp, windless wave that I felt like I was surrounded by walls of glass. I could see the sun right through the wave. I could see the seaweed too and the rocks below. And then, there, just inches away, but inside the wall of glass, the seal pup. He was tracking me inside the wave as I raced across.

The whole thing was so bloody beautiful, I mean, so outrageously whopping mind-blowing that I lost control altogether. The wave sucked me up into the collapsing tube and knocked me off my board. Then it slammed down on my head and rolled me around in a mass of frigid white water.

I came up hungry for air and my head hurt from the cold. It's what we call an ice cream headache. But there was the seal pup looking at me like we were long lost buddies. And there was my board, only a few feet away, still tied to me by the leash. Despite the cold, the sun felt warm on my face as I blinked out the water.

I had just about got my breath and my sanity back. I was pulling myself up onto my board when another wave sucked me up into its throat. I had been wrong. There were six waves in the set, not five.

I didn't have a chance to dive deep. It threw me over the falls and bounced me right off a rock, one of those big round boulders near the shore. It almost knocked the wind out of me, but I just rolled right off it and came up gulping for air again.

The seal was gone, out to safer, deeper water. I was all alone now, my head stinging again from the cold. But I didn't care. I knew that this was as good as it got and that this was the way it was going to be for a long time to come.

Sixteen years old had freedom written all over it.

Chapter Two

My Learner's Permit

When Kevin got back in with the boat, he took me to Halifax to get my learner's permit.

"Rand, why don't you give up on school and come work on the boat with me? With two of us, we could make good money. They wouldn't mind."

"They" meant our parents. It was probably true. They let Kevin quit early when my old man stopped going to sea. My father gave Kevin his boat and fishing license and opened up the welding shop around back. Now we have a back yard full of rusty iron scraps of all sorts and maybe fifteen junk cars that he's never got around to fixing.

"I don't want to quit school," I told Kevin, even though I had maybe a hundred good reasons to quit.

Kev just sort of scowled into the windshield. He pulled his Moosehead cap down low in the front, rolled down the window and spit a big hocker out into the street. Then he let out a long, low belch like he'd been saving it up for just this conversation.

I rolled down my window and looked out at the traffic on Robie Street. I saw kids on the side street popping wheelies on their BMX bikes. I saw a guy wearing expensive shades and a Beaver Canoe sweatshirt sitting on a bench with his arm around a girl who looked like she just stepped out of a movie. I knew why I didn't want to quit school. I didn't want to be like Kevin.

"Kevin, man, you're gross."

"And you're fat," he snapped back. Great. Now we had reverted to being little brats again.

"What's the point of school, anyway?" he said. "You're not going to make better money than fishing."

"Yeah, then how come you're not rolling in it?"

"It's been a bad year. Fish'll come back."

"Yeah, but I don't like fish. They stink. And they're slimy and you have to go way out in the ocean every morning to catch the damn things."

"I thought you didn't mind going out in the ocean on your little surfboard to play around with the waves."

"That's different," I said. We were stopped at the light on Young Street trying to make a left hand turn. When the light went green, Kevin floored it, squealing tires and sneaking across the oncoming traffic. A couple of cars blew horns at him and one driver had to slam on his brakes. Kevin just laughed.

I just barely scraped by the written driver's test. I think if I had had one more wrong, they wouldn't have given me the permit.

"You should have studied your book more carefully," a cranky examiner told me. "If it was up to me, I'd say go home and do it again."

I tried to smile politely at the insult. I really wanted to say something gross back, but all I could manage was a grunt. What she didn't know was that I had stayed up late every night for a week studying the speed limits and the meaning of the idiot signs, and what the fines were, and all that jazz. But some-how it wouldn't sink in, just like every other thing I ever tried to learn. So in the end I scraped by ... as always. That was the story of my life. If I had a dollar for every test that I nearly flunked I'd be a rich man.

I waited for the woman behind the desk to hand over my permit. Out in the parking lot I could see Kevin waiting in his car. His old Ford was the most beat-up looking thing in the parking lot. That is typical of my family. Suddenly I felt kind of sorry for him. I realized again that I didn't want to be like him.

I didn't say thank you when she handed over the papers. Two feet out the door, I nearly walked into the side of an RCMP car that was just pulling up. I found myself apologizing to the fender.

The door opened and the driver got out. At first, all I saw was uniform, but then I noticed the cop was a woman.

"Darlene?"

"Yeah, your mom told me you were here getting your license. So I came to congratulate you."

I guess I looked a little wimped-out just then.

"You did pass, didn't you?"

"Just barely."

"Good, let's celebrate. I'm off work in about fifteen minutes."

It wasn't what I expected to hear from a lady Mountie. But Darlene was no ordinary Mountie. She and I went way back. She was the only one in my entire family of thirty-five relatives that I could ever relate to. A cousin — my favourite one. I shouldn't admit this, but I used to have a crush on her.

"Celebrate?" I asked.

"Pizza," she said. "On me. You only turn sixteen once in your life."

Yeah, like I really need the extra calories, I heard myself thinking. "Sure. I'll get Kevin."

She followed me over to my brother's heap. I roused Kevin from a pretend sleep. His radio was up full blast with his Alabama tape.

"Free pizza," I said, pointing at Darlene.

Kevin took one look at the uniform. He had a thing against Mounties ever since they took his license away for six months for drunk driving. "No way," he said. "Let's go home. You pass or what?"

I felt caught in the middle of something. I had to choose.

"I'll give you a ride back down the shore if you like, Randy. I want to go see my folks in Seaforth, anyway," said Darlene.

I looked at Kevin. He had given me the ride here. And he was probably going to let me drive on the way home, once we got past the Penhorn Mall. He was being generous. Why the heck should I have to insult somebody here?

Kevin took one look at me and fired up the car. "See you at home," he said, his voice hard as nails. He ground the gears into reverse and spit gravel as he backed out of the parking spot, then shot away.

"Double cheese, mushrooms, peppers, pepperoni and anchovies," Darlene said, trying to bring some spirit back into me.

Blubber belly, I could hear the kids from school call me. Yeah, I figured, so what? "No anchovies," I said, "I hate fish."

Chapter Three

Invasion of the Townies

By the crack of June I had my driver's license. You guessed it, I just barely squeaked by. You see, I was still having a hard time with the clutch on Kevin's Ford. I forgot to put on a turn signal once and I had to have three tries at parallel parking. It was pretty frustrating. I mean, there wasn't even any place to parallel park on the Eastern Shore that I knew of. Why the heck did I have to learn that?

But the guy with the clipboard beside me seemed pretty easy-going and let me pass. When I got home, there was my mom waiting for me. "I got a surprise for you, Rankle. Close your eyes and follow me into the back yard," she said.

At first I thought she was just goofing on me. But I let her lead me around back and didn't even open my eyes when I heard the garage door to my old man's shop roll up.

"Open," she said.

I opened my eyes. But I didn't see anything unusual. It was just my dad's crummy welding shop with another old clunker up on blocks sitting inside.

"What do you think?" Kevin asked.

"Holy smokes," I said.

"It's yours," my old man said, sounding pleased as punch.

"Mine?" Now I recognized it — the old rusty Chevette that Fred Myatt had rolled off the road and then given to my father for parts. My father had bashed out most of the dents and you could see that he had welded on new metal in two or three places. It was finished off in a dull grey primer paint.

"You fixed this up for me?" I asked. I knew that I couldn't be caught dead driving this wreck.

"Kevin helped," my dad said. "We only worked on her when you were in school. Then we rolled her out and kept a tarp on her. Some hard keeping it a secret from you, son."

I was trapped. What could I do? "Thanks, guys," I said. "Man, my own wheels. This is great."

I don't think my mom or dad could see through it. But I knew that Kevin did. And I knew that I had really hurt his feelings.

The next day warmed up to something almost like summer. A low-pressure system offshore had sent in a new swell and I could see out my window the white water at the point. I drove my "new" car over with my board on top and pulled up behind the barrier rocks at the beach. I expected to see Chris or Reggie, or some of the older guys, but it was still too early in the day and I guess most of them were working.

Instead, what I found was really weird.

There were three cars there. One had a hatchback open with big speakers blasting out music. Wetsuit gear and surf wax and towels and all kinds of junk were lying all over the ground. And in the water were maybe twelve guys on those short foam boards — a bunch of boogie boarders who looked like they had no idea as to how to catch a wave, and out at the point, guys on surfboards, catching the shoulder of waves and falling right off.

I felt like someone had just yanked the rug out from under me. Where'd they come from?

I guess I was just sort of standing there with my jaw dropped down about two feet when one of the boogie boarders comes out of the water. He kicks off his flippers and runs up the beach, climbs over the rocks and throws the boogie board down on the ground. He's got his back to me and I can see he's got long straggly wet hair like an old hippy. I walk towards him, curious as hell to find out what's going on. I mean, like this is my spot. Aside from the older guys who taught me to surf, this is my beach. Those are my waves. I know I don't have any right to own the place, but I feel threatened, angry.

"How's the water?" I asked. I meant the temperature.

"Cold," he said. But it wasn't a he. It was a she. And as she turned around, I was completely knocked out because she was standing there in a very tight black and pink wetsuit, and I'd never even seen a girl in a wetsuit before. I was stunned.

"Going surfing?" she asked.

"Well, yeah." Why was it that suddenly I felt like the fat lump again, the too tall, blubbery kid that I turned into every time I walked through the door at school? This was my beach, my world. They all had no right here. Not even her. My life was ruined.

"That was my first time," she said.

"You with them?" I pointed towards the other guys sitting on their surfboards in the water. I didn't recognize any of them. I just knew they weren't from the Shore. They were townies.

CONTENTS

"Sort of," she said.

"Where you from?"

"Halifax. I'm Cathy. Brian just had all the gear shipped up from Florida. Some tri-fins, a few quads, some O'Neill suits and a few boogie boards. You surf here often?"

"All the time," I said. I know I sounded kind of tough right then but then she melted me down real quick.

"Good, then maybe I'll see you quite a bit. Brian, my boyfriend, he'll probably spend hours in the water. I'm only good for about twenty minutes. Feel that." She held out her arm. I took her hand.

"Cold," I said.

"It's like numb. Your hand feels nice and warm."

I drew my hand back, wiped the sea water off on my pants.

"Well, see ya," I said and turned toward my car. I decided I was going to drive home. It was all too weird for me. But as I started up, she yelled at me, "Aren't you going out? The waves are great."

I turned off the engine. Yeah, she was right. What the heck was wrong with me? I had come to go surfing. As carefully as I could, I put my wetsuit on inside my little car. I could see her in the rear view mirror looking towards me. I think she was laughing.

When I had my gear on, I climbed over the rocks, avoiding her, and began paddling out to the point, past the boogie boarders in the shore break.

"Hot waves, dude," somebody said to me. It was innocent enough, but it was the way he said it. I felt like someone had just stolen something very precious from me.

The six guys at the point all had brand new boards and hot-looking wetsuits. I had on an old diving suit and the only board I'd ever owned. It had plenty of patched up dings. Reggie, an older guy who taught me to surf when I was a kid, gave me the board. I guess I'm kind of attached to it.

I tried to avoid the townies but they paddled right over.

"Can you rip with that old thing, or what?" one guy asked. Somebody else laughed. I felt like part of some freak show.

I didn't answer, just paddled for the first wave coming. Two other guys tried to catch it but neither could get up the speed. I made it, though. I dropped down the face of it just in time to get nailed by the lip of water and thrashed around on the bottom.

When I came back up, I heard hoots and laughing. "Yeah, man, go for it," somebody said. "You should have been a bit further outside."

Boy was I mad. Who were these turkeys who had probably never been in waves outside of a bathtub? Who were they to be giving me advice?

But I paddled a little further outside, picked the right wave, a fully stoked overhead peak and dropped down the face of it right through the small knot of other surfers. I didn't hit anyone, but I could see them all get sucked over the falls as I sneaked past the peak and out onto the shoulder. They were in the water scrambling for boards as I did a roundhouse cutback way out on the shoulder, drove back into the lip and did a floater down across the whitewater, then kicked high up into the thin lip and bashed it right up into the air, for an aerial exit.

This time, they hooted again.

I paddled straight back out and repeated the performance three more times. At that point, one of the guys who had been nailed by nearly as many waves and was having a hard time just getting back out, came over.

"Good stuff," he said. "My name's Brian. I guess you really can rip on that old board, after all. Mind giving me a few pointers?" Brian was a muscular, skinny guy, about my age. It registered that this was Cathy's boyfriend. I thought of her on the beach. I looked at the townies in the water and the boogie boarders in by shore. How had it all changed so quick? Maybe they'd all go away. Maybe they'd get frustrated and never come back.

"Sure," I said. "But I have to go in now. Catch you next time."

"Sure thing, bro," Brian said and paddled off toward his buddies.

Chapter Four

Cathy

To get in to shore, I had to drop in on a couple of the boogie boarders — you know, foamheads. These guys clearly had no idea what they were doing in the water. I should have just gone to shore another way, but I kind of liked the feel of blasting past them and seeing them get dunked as they tried to get out of my way. None of them seemed to mind.

On shore, I climbed over the rocks again and walked to my slate grey Chevette. Some of the townies hanging out by their cars were looking at me. They were laughing. It's hard to say whether they were laughing at me or at my wheels. I mean we both were pretty pathetic to look at. Forget them.

I had to get out of my soggy wetsuit before I drove home. Otherwise the driver's seat would sop up all the salt water and stay wet for maybe the next two weeks.

Usually this changing business wouldn't be a problem. I mean, in the old days — you know, before I could drive, I'd just ride home on my bicycle with my board under my arm. I think it looked really bizarre to people driving by. Once a gust of wind caught my board like a sail and we got whipped off the road into the ditch.

But now I had a car. And besides, usually there was no one around this end of the beach. If I wanted to, I could just whip off my wetsuit and peel down to the bare essentials right by the side of the road. There wasn't that much traffic. The worst I could do was moon some little old lady driving home from the Superstore.

So there I was surrounded by townies and foam-heads and I didn't really think I could successfully yank myself out of my soggy one-piece wetsuit while sitting in the front seat of my tiny Chevette. And, like I need to admit that I didn't have anything on under-neath of my wetsuit. To tell you the truth, I don't even own swimming trunks. I never really just swim in the ocean and whenever I surf or body surf, I always wear a wetsuit. My mother's never bought me swim trunks and I guess I just never got around to it.

And now you're getting the picture. There I am, leaning against the car, pulling one arm and then the other out of my wetsuit. Believe me, this is a real ordeal. In order for a suit to keep you warm it has to be tight. Mine was. And so maybe I had put on a couple of extra pounds lately. Well, the whole busi-ness was like wrestling with a killer squid, if you get my drift.

I pulled down the zipper, got the shoulders pulled down and got the arms inside out but got stuck with both my hands still trapped in the arms. It was kind of like I was handcuffed. And it seemed that no matter which way I wrenched myself, I couldn't get either of my hands free. To top it off, I could see that I had a very keen audience. I felt my face turning red. Boy, did I want to get out of there.

I probably looked like a lunatic, just flailing a-round with my suit half down and arms still stuck in the suit. Just then somebody came up from behind me.

"Want some help?"

I spun around to see who it was. That girl. Cathy. Oh, man, this was just great. I was sure she would think I was an idiot.

She began to pull on one of the sleeves until one hand popped free. "I saw you catch some decent waves out there. How long have you been surfing?"

"Since I was twelve," I said, pulling my other arm free. Twelve, yeah. She probably figured from the way I was acting that I was all of thirteen.

"Well, I've never quite seen anything like that in Nova Scotia before."

As I mentioned, this Cathy was really a knockout. She had on this pullover windbreaker and short pants and sandals and it seemed like she was really out of place here because the kind of women I usually saw at the beach this early in the year were little old blue-haired ladies in tennis sneakers who walked their dogs up and down the beach and looked for shells.

I guess I thought she'd just walk away but she didn't. She just leaned against my car looking at me.

Yeah, me, with the top half of my blubber body for all the world to see. And, as you might figure, I had this other problem. How the hell could I get out of the rest of my suit with her standing there?

"Do you need some help getting that thing off the rest of the way?"

"No," I said nervously. "I can do it."

She looked out to sea. "You know, there's some-thing about this place. I can't quite pin it down, but there seems to be so much life, so much power from the ocean. It, like, makes you feel high just from being here."

"I know just what you mean."

"Maybe it's just the negative ions."

"The what?"

"Negative ions. They say there are more negative ions in the air along the shoreline. And negative ions make people feel more up than down."

"If you say so." I knew I was in over my head.

I could see that Brian had paddled in. He had a strong, easy, swimmer's stroke. He was new at surfing, but I could tell from the way he could paddle that, once he got the hang of it, he'd be a natural. Before too long, he'd be hot. And that bothered me.

Brian shook his head like a dog would as he got out of the water, then ran and hopped up over the rocks to where we stood.

At first, it seemed that I was invisible to him. "Hey, babe, get that zipper, okay?"

Brian had one of those suits with a long zipper across the back. Cathy immediately did as she was told and that made me feel pretty ugly. Brian popped his head through the neck seal and shook his hair again. Cathy pulled a pair of designer sunglasses out of her back pocket and put them on Brian.

I was thinking, what was this? The guy couldn't stand being on dry land for over three minutes without having on fancy shades ... what a jerk. Then he did the unforgivable. "Cathy, would you mind taking my board back to the car and strapping it on the rack. I'll be there in a minute and we can split. Maybe we can catch a donair on the way home, whaddya say?"

"Sure," she said, smiling. She picked up his board and carried it away.

Brian stood there for a minute, just staring out to sea with his shades on like he was posing for a photograph for *SURFER* magazine. "What's your name, pal?"

"Randy."

"Good to meet you, Randy. Man, I hope you'll be good enough to help me figure out this sport. I've only surfed a couple of times before when my old man took me to L.A. but I've got a lot to learn. Promise you'll give me some coaching?"

It wasn't what I expected to hear. This guy was actually being nice to me. Who was I to turn down a friend? I didn't have any to speak of except for Darlene … who was really my cousin and much older, and a few of the regular surfers who were busy most of the time with jobs. Yeah, maybe a friend like Brian was just what I needed. "Sure, man, anytime."

"That's cool," he said. He punched me lightly on the shoulder and walked away.

I still didn't know how to get out of my wetsuit without being seen, so I just sat down at the steering wheel and drove off, knowing I'd have a squishy seat for a long time. Then, halfway down the road, the glow of Brian being nice to me wore off. I thought about Cathy. I wasn't sure, but I think the girl had really liked me. The more I thought about it, the more I was sure of it. But then what about the way Brian had just jumped up out of the water and began ordering her around like he owned her?

Now that made me bloody angry. Yeah, I thought, when Cathy's back was turned, I should have finished taking off my wetsuit right there by the side of the road. If I had had a chance to think it through, I should have mooned that guy Brian right then and there.

Chapter Five

Never on Dry Land

It was my last day of school for the year — the day we went in to pick up our report cards. I was a little surprised that Mr. Haines, the hard-nosed math teacher who hassled me all the time, didn't flunk me. He let me slip by with a D. He must have had a soft spot in his heart after all. In fact, it turned out that I just squeaked by in most of my subjects. Was I ever glad that year was over. It was behind me. And now I had nothing ahead of me but summer, which meant waves.

I had my little Chev parked on the street by the school and when I got in, George and Poker pulled up alongside in Poker's jacked-up Jeep.

Poker rolled down the window and blew some cigarette smoke at me. "Rankle, George here says you're too wimped to even race us from here to the stop sign. He says he'll give you five bucks if you can come in even one car-length behind me."

I shook my head. It seemed like somebody was always trying to goof on me. What was I going to do in my old Chevette? I had a full 1.6 litres of engine power under there. Enough to maybe power an electric tooth brush. I just shook my head in disgust.

"Not even willing to try?" George asked.

I looked into the windshield for a second. What was it about me anyway that made turkeys like them want to give me a hard time? "Bug off," I said. I turned the ignition on, pretended I was ignoring them, then let the clutch pedal go and floored it. There was a tiny squelch of rubber. The stop sign was about half a kilometre away. Kids were walking down the side of the road and didn't notice anything until they heard the roar of Poker's Jeep as he pushed the pedal through the floorboards.

All I had going for me was a head start. That didn't last long. Poker slipped past like a bullet and there I was over-revving my engine in second gear, trying to catch up. Everybody was watching.

It was too short a distance to really get up any speed but Poker had given it all he had. He had to slam on the brakes at the stop sign, and even at that he skidded halfway out into the oncoming traffic. I pushed it hard to the end but I was more than two car-lengths behind. I had to hit my brakes hard and when I came to a stop my engine stalled.

Poker backed up and he and George just smiled. "You owe us five bills," George said.

"I didn't agree to any bet," I shouted. I cranked my engine over to get it to start but it wouldn't go. Either my starter was jammed again or the battery was dead.

All the local kids were walking by getting a good grin out of it. George and Poker took off. I could see they were pleased with their bit of entertainment at my expense.

My old man didn't seem too unhappy with my report card but my mom said, "You could have done better.

You should try harder if you wanna be something."
That was one of her usual lines.

What did I exactly want to be?

"Randy," Kevin said, "I could still use you on the
boat. No more school for an excuse now. If you don't
want to do it, I'll hire the Robicheau kid."

I knew this was coming.

"You better take him up on it, Randy, " my old man
said. "You need money to keep that car running. And
you've got insurance on it to think of. I can't keep it
on my policy or those snoops will catch up with me."

"Your father's right," my mother said.

"Okay," I said. "Three mornings a week." I didn't
want to go at all. I'd rather go to town and get some
job working at K-Mart but I hoped this would make
them happy.

"The boy's just plain lazy," my old man said. He
could see that I really didn't want to do it. I could see
he was getting angry. Kevin should have been mad at
me too but he just shook his head.

"We'll give it a try," he said, "and see how it works
out."

I knew that Kevin was a much better brother to
me than I was to him but I didn't know how to let him
know that. My father's words kept echoing in my head
… *just plain lazy* … and what else could somebody
say? *Lazy and stupid and fat and* … the list could go
on and on.

I had about an hour of light left before dark so I
grabbed my board out of the yard and drove over to
the beach. There were a few cars parked but nobody
was in the water. I paddled out to some mediocre
four-foot waves and caught a few rides. It was nothing
special but a chance to clear my head and feel human

again. Maybe I didn't belong on dry land at all, I thought, as a big old grey seal popped up several yards away. There was a loon nearby too, not to mention a couple of feisty fish that kept jumping up to catch the bugs.

I didn't need big waves to feel good in the ocean. I just needed this. I had a few easy rides, then I tried something.

I took off with my eyes closed. I let myself feel the wave without seeing it. I turned left, leaned into the wall, shot down the line, punched my head right into the wall of the wave, and did a head dip before kicking out. Never once had I opened my eyes. No problem. I had my systems down that perfect.

I didn't even open my eyes until I heard somebody blow a car horn. There was some idiot driving a four-by-four on the grass high up on the headland. I should have known. Poker and George had driven out from Cole Harbour and they were now parked right at the edge of the dirt cliff. George yelled something down to me about coming to collect his five bucks.

I tried to ignore them. I could see they were drinking beer and when they had finished, both of them heaved their bottles down the cliff where they broke into a thousand pieces on the rocks. Next, those two jerks started heaving some other garbage, including an empty beer box. Poker put it in gear and sped off along the rim of the headland, tearing up the grass. When he was back on the highway, he blasted on his horn a few more times before heading up the hill and back to town.

I paddled back in. The spell had been broken.

Chapter Six

Surfers Not Wanted

A couple of days later Darlene came over to the house. It was pretty weird. She was wearing her uniform and it made my old man and Kevin pretty uncomfortable. Leave it to my mom to just blurt out, "For the love of God, you men! Just 'cause Darlene's got her working clothes on, don't mean she's any different."

Then my mom poured everybody tea. My father started for the cabinet with the rum bottle 'cause he'd offer a little drop of rum with the tea when family came calling but he stopped halfway, turned and smiled at Darlene.

"Just a drop," Darlene said, "I'm off duty." And I knew she said it just to put my old man at ease.

After a while, Kevin drifted off to watch TV and my dad went out back to finish welding the chassis of Hanford McDermid's Pontiac. Even my mom faded off to listen to the CBC radio news in the other room.

"So how's it going?" Darlene asked.

"It's like great and it's terrible," I told her. This was just like old times. When Darlene was in high school and I was still a fat little brat in grade school, she was about the only one who could ever sit down and talk to me like this, like I really mattered.

And if it wasn't for Darlene, I'd probably never have had a chance to surf. I know that sounds crazy but back then when I was only twelve years old, she was going out with Reggie, the guy who gave me his old board. His friend Chris was going to give me a wetsuit. They got a kick out of the idea of a fat little kid like me learning to surf. My mom said no way, that I'd get myself drowned out there. My old man said the whole thing didn't make one lick of sense.

But good old Darlene sat down at the kitchen table and told them straight out that this could be the most important thing that ever happened to me ... that I needed to surf.

And they listened to her.

Later, we all thought she was loony for wanting to go into the RCMP. This could be a pretty tough shore and the idea of a woman trying to break up a brawl at the Downeaster or trying to arrest Jimmy Robicheau or Rupert Preston for drunk driving just sounded right crazy. But not to Darlene who just went right ahead and did it. She breezed into the job like nothing to it.

Darlene studied the confusion in my face, "You're not in love are you?" she asked.

"What?" I was really freaked by the question. "That's the stupidest thing I ever heard. Where'd you get an idea like that?" I heard myself just about shouting at her.

"Sorry, I'm no expert. I just sort of had this hunch."

"Well, your hunch is wrong. Dead wrong," I heard myself saying. I looked down at the wood grain on the table and at the cigarette burn left there by Alicia Purdy on New Year's Eve.

"Just thought I'd ask."

"Well, it's personal," I said, sounding very protective. But as I said it, I knew I was admitting something to Darlene and to myself. I wasn't just staring at a cigarette burn on the wooden table top. There was this image of Cathy floating before me, the same darn image that had been stuck in my head for days now. What was going on?

"Okay, I'll change the subject," Darlene said. "How have the waves been?"

"Good," I answered flatly.

"Okay, so you don't want to talk about that either." She was looking a little frustrated. I couldn't understand why I was being so cold to her. It was just that I was so darned confused.

"Randy, there was something I came to let you know about. You know that the province is turning the beach into a provincial park, right?"

"Yeah, I guess I heard that."

"Well, the park developers sent us a copy of the proposed plan for our input and I thought you should know about a few things."

I didn't know what she was getting at.

"They want to put up a guard rail near the headland. It'll close off that end of the beach for parking."

"How am I supposed to get to the waves?"

"Well, they're opening up a big parking lot midway down the beach. You'll just have to walk back there, I guess."

"That stinks. We've always been able to park where we surf. It's not fair."

"I know, but here's the kicker. The official parking lot will have a gate across and it'll be locked. They'll have someone open it at nine o'clock and close it again at eight at night."

"But I get in the water earlier than that and sometimes in the summer, I stay in the water until dark — eight-thirty, sometimes nine."

"It gets worse. The parking lot will be open only from May to October. Unless you want to walk there from here, you're not going to be able to park legally anywhere along there."

Life just seemed to be full of one headache after another. Somehow I got the impression that there were people out there who just sat around devising ways to make my life miserable. "Why?" I asked. "Why are they doing this to me?"

Darlene looked like she felt sorry for me. "I'm not sure. Maybe you should ask the planners. I guess they have this idea as to what sort of a place Lawrencetown Beach should be and surfers just don't seem to fit in. I don't know the whole story but I do know that somebody — a tourist I think, phoned my dispatcher at work the other day complaining about kids hanging out there and playing loud music and being a nuisance. She said they had surfboards. The same lady phoned back the next day to say that somebody in four-by-four was driving up along the headland tearing up the land and throwing around beer bottles. I guess this leads somebody to the conclusion that surfers just aren't very nice people."

Chapter Seven

Goofy Footers Unite

I started getting up in the dark to go out on my brother's boat. It wasn't so bad, really. I liked watching the sun come up at sea and we'd cruise past the headland so I'd get a chance to see how the waves were breaking. I wanted to take my board along, maybe drop off and get a few rides while Kev hauled in lobster traps or hand lines.

"No way," Kevin told me.

"Bull!" I said, but it was his boat so he had the final say.

I'd get home, eat some lunch and get to the beach by about one, just in time for the townies and foam-heads to show up. Cathy would be there and she'd wave to me but most of the time I felt too chicken to just sit down and talk to her.

I didn't know how to tell the townies about the problem with the new park, that we were all going to get kicked out of parking near the headland. In fact, I didn't want to think about it. I tried avoiding Brian and his crowd but it seemed like every time I took off on a wave, someone was dropping in on me.

Finally, I got so ticked off, I paddled over to Brian and told him this: "Look, there's not really any rules out here but there is this sort of unwritten law, that the guy who takes off on a wave who's closest to the curl has the right of way."

Brian gave me this freaked-out look. So did two of his buddies — a guy they called Belcher and a wiry redhead named Fitz. I expected they were all about to have a good laugh at my little lecture. Instead, Brian said, "So, at last the famous hotshot surf dude speaks."

I didn't say anything. I felt pretty stupid.

"Why didn't you tell me that before? I can take a hint," Brian said. "I mean, just because you know how to rip and shred these waves doesn't mean you have to be so damn stuck-up."

Stuck-up, me? Brian seemed to be taking me seriously. Heck, I figured he'd come over and slug me one.

"Tell me more about unwritten laws," he said.

"Well, like there are usually enough waves to go around so if there's a bunch of guys out, you sort of take turns."

"Like ... take a number, right?"

"Sort of."

"Sounds fair to me," he said. This was not what I was expecting. "Look, man, we just figured you hated our guts, like we were invading your territory but maybe we can be buddies after all."

"Yeah?"

"Randy, you pull moves on waves we could only dream of. What do you say to teaching me a few things?"

"Sure, why not."

"All right. First lesson. How come that when I take off on a wave, I get to the bottom, go to turn and nothing happens. I go splat on the water and get gobbled?"

"You're not making the bottom turn. I see what you're doing. You just gotta get your back foot further back, right over the fins."

He smiled. I think it made sense to him. A set was coming. Brian wanted to try out the advice. He was closer to the peak than I was and began to paddle hard. The other guys just sat and watched. Then he stopped. "Oh, sorry. Your wave?"

"No man. Your wave. Go for it."

He paddled like a mad man. Then he was up. He hesitated for a second but then I saw he got his leg back further, his foot was almost on the tail. When he leaned into the wave, he discovered that he had kicked a beautiful bottom turn and was arcing high up onto the little wall of water. He was in position and steaming down the line like an old pro. He let out a yelp and the other guys cheered.

From then on, the townies treated me like a best buddy. Brian kept asking me questions. I'd show him how I did it and they'd all be pretty impressed. By early July, it felt pretty good to be in the water with a bunch of guys who hung on my every word. They were all learning quick. And if I wanted a wave, people would back off and let me have it.

The waves were getting small and lazy so I didn't stay in the water much over an hour. The other guys would stay with it. They were new and would surf any old junk that came along. I was getting picky in my old age.

That's when this other stuff started happening. One day I paddled in and sat down on my board on the beach. I had thought a lot about Cathy but I knew she was Brian's girlfriend and I didn't want to fool around with our friendship. But this day was down-right hot. No wind at all. I just wanted to sit there on the beach and soak up the sun. Cathy saw me and walked over.

"Can I sit down?"

"Sure." I could feel myself getting all nervous. I knew I'd make a goof if I even moved so I was probably even holding my breath.

She sat down on my board just inches from me and began to stir the sand with a stick. "What do you think of Brian?" she asked.

"He's okay," I said. "He's getting pretty good. I never learned that quick. Soon, he'll be thrashing up the place out there."

"I wasn't asking what you thought of him as a surfer. I mean, what do you think of him as a … a human being?"

I didn't know what she meant by that. It sounded kind of philosophical. I picked up a stick and began to make circles in the sand, just like Cathy. "I don't know," I said. "I guess he's okay as a human being," but I could tell by the way I said it that it sounded pretty stupid.

She began to laugh. And even though I think she was laughing at me, I rather liked it. So I went for it. "But I'll tell you one thing I bet you didn't know about him."

"What's that?"

"He's not a goofy foot."

"What?"

"He surfs with his left foot forward, like most people. But I surf with my right foot forward. It's called being goofy foot. We goofy footers are a minority in the surf world. What about you?"

"I don't know," she said. She gave me the cutest smile and suddenly I remembered Darlene's question from a few weeks back. Maybe I wasn't in love with Cathy back then, just interested. But now it was different. I was definitely in love. My heart was pounding like sledge hammer.

"Okay. Well just stand here on my surfboard."

"There. How's that?"

"Is that the way that feels most comfortable to you?"

"Yeah."

"Then you're a goofy foot. You're like me."

"That's good. Then we have something in common. We're goofy feet."

I think I must've turned beet red just then.

"You're lucky that you live out here," Cathy said. "There's something about this place, some quality, that makes me feel more alive when I'm here. I hope this place will never change."

"Yeah, me too," I said, thinking about how it was already changing ... too fast and not at all for the good. "But we might not be able to stop it. We already have idiots who come out here and tear up the headland and the dunes with cars and motorcycles and now we have parks people who want to turn this place into a park. If they have their way, they'll figure out a way to kick surfers out of here altogether. It's happened that way all over North America."

Cathy shook her head. "It's all wrong. This *is* a very special place. Those waves ... I know why they're better here than anywhere along the coast."

"You do?" This was unexpected. How did she know anything about waves?

"My dad has ocean charts. I took a look. The water is deep closer to shore here than just about anywhere.

No islands to block off incoming swells either. So if you have like a major low-pressure system out there anywhere, the waves roll unobstructed hundreds of miles until they make it here."

"Wow," was all I could say. She was right. Reggie had explained the same thing to me years ago but I couldn't believe this was coming from ... well, from a girl.

"And there's something else. Look."

I looked to where she was pointing. Several small, familiar shore birds were running on spindly legs near the shoreline.

"Piping plovers," Cathy said. "An endangered species. Not that many left in the world. And if we're not careful — either your 'idiots' with their cars and bikes or the park developers might destroy them. Once they're scared off from here, they might not come back ever."

"That'll never happen," I said, trying to keep her from getting too bummed out.

"Why?"

"'Cause the goofy footers won't let it." And I looked straight into her eyes and without opening my mouth tried to tell her the way I really felt about her just then.

And I guess that that was the real beginning of the Cathy thing. At first, I thought she was just beautiful but then I learned she was into all sorts of stuff. She said she took pictures, so I asked her to bring her camera out. We'd walk up and down the beach and to the top of the headland and taking close-up pictures of all sorts of neat, strange stuff like seaweed and driftwood that looked like dragons, even just rocks. Then one day she said, "Here. You take a picture of something that you think is really interesting."

I fooled with the focus on the lens and found out that you could get right close to anything. And so I took a picture of her big toe. On purpose. Yeah, I thought everything about Cathy was so perfect that I was even in love with her big toe. I couldn't say that because I was afraid she'd stop hanging out with me. I was holding onto this fantasy that she had a crush on me but I knew that was impossible.

When she had the film developed, she gave me a large colour blow up of her big toe. I said it was the neatest photograph I ever owned. That was when she leaned over and gave me a kiss on the cheek. I could have died and gone to heaven right then.

"You're not at all like Brian," she said.

"How do you mean that?"

"Well, like he's always ordering me around. *Do this, do that.* And he takes me for granted. I'm just his little beach bunny hanging out on the beach. Sometimes I like it okay. Other times I don't."

"Brian's okay," I said. In the water Brian still treated me like his best friend. As soon as we were on dry land, though, he turned back into his other self. He ignored me, ordered Cathy around and always had to be the centre of attention.

"Sometimes he's okay," she said. "He's cute and he takes me out places I'd never get to go to. I guess he's all right."

And then, speak of the devil, there was Brian running up the beach and dripping water all over us. I had to wipe off the drops from the photograph.

"What's that, Ran?" he asked.

"A picture," I said. I didn't want him to see it. I tried to hide it but he got ticked off. "Let me see it," he ordered.

Cathy handed it to him. "It's a picture Randy took. Very artistic, I'd say."

"It's somebody's toe," Brian said, laughing.

"It's my toe," Cathy answered angrily. "And Randy thinks it's beautiful."

Brian shook more water off his hair all over us. "I need some wax, Cathy. Would you mind going up to the car to get me some."

Cathy gave me a look of defeat. "Sure," she said.

As soon as she was over the rocks, Brian took the photograph and ripped it into little pieces and tossed it in the wind. I was so mad I could have punched him in the face right there. But Cathy came back with the bar of surf wax, threw a towel around Brian's shoulders, and began rubbing his neck with it. I just picked up my board and left, feeling like someone had just stuck a knife in my chest and given it a hard twist.

Chapter Eight

Nothing But Hassles

After that, Brian didn't seem so friendly. Belcher and Fitz left me alone, too. They all could surf now and were picking up new tricks each time out. I tried being friendly but apparently the word was out that I was no longer one of the boys.

Trying to sort this all out in my mind, it seemed to mean only one thing. Brian was actually jealous of me. Unbelievable but true. And he had turned the other guys against me as well.

A nice smooth shoulder-high peak was headed towards me. Brian and I both paddled. He was inside. It should have been his wave only I didn't back off. He dropped to the bottom and I cut high and stayed just above him on the wave. I went out on the shoulder, pulled a roundhouse and came back right at him. I wasn't trying to hit him. I just felt like showing off. But before I knew what happened, Brian had grabbed the nose of my board and knocked me off the back of the wave. He zipped on past like nothing had happened.

When he returned, I didn't say anything.

"Sorry about that," he told me, his face expressionless.

"It's okay," I heard myself say. "It was your wave."

I caught a sloppy dumper of a wave and paddled for shore. On the beach, a few of the foamheads and a couple of townie surfers whose names I didn't know were sitting in their cars. Music was blasting out. I watched somebody finish off a Big Mac and a Coke, then throw the wrappers and bottle on the ground. I was already ticked-off because of Brian and this grossed me out, so I had to say something.

"Pick it up," I said to a little mongrel thirteen-year-old with designer sunglasses and a green zinc-oxide nose.

"Why? It won't hurt anyone."

"Yeah, it does hurt. This is a beautiful place and people like me who live here don't like to see it screwed up." I sounded like a freaking teacher or something. I could see the kids in the car all making funny faces like they thought this was a big joke. That really made me feel burned.

"You mean, like you *live* out here in the sticks?" he asked in a nervy little brat voice. "What do people out here do for a living?" he asked. "Fish?" And all the little goofs cracked up.

I grabbed the little twerp by his collar and lifted him out of his car. "Pick it up," I said.

He did. But when I walked back to my car I could see they all thought this was a riot. I couldn't hear what they said but I got the general idea. I knew that they all thought I was pretty stale, all these little goofs from the south end of Halifax or whatever. Their parents just gave them money to burn. They thought I was a hick. Why had I ever been so stupid to think that I was one of them? And what right did they have to come here and surf my waves in my ocean?

In my Chevette I found Cathy sitting in the front seat. "I just wanted to get in out of the sun," she said.

"Hi."

"I saw that," she said. "You're right. I'm with you. I walk around and pick up trash sometimes when you guys are out surfing. I don't mind."

"Yeah, but somebody's gotta teach them a little respect." Suddenly I sounded like my old man.

"Go easy, they're just kids."

"Right," I said.

I felt like a big slob again. I knew that I had been used by Brian. I might as well hang up my board and wait for fall so all the townies would clear out. But there was this other thing. I didn't know why Cathy was sitting in my car. Maybe Brian had locked his and not given her the keys. Maybe not.

"Cathy, would you like go out with me or something?" I asked her point blank. If I had given myself a chance to think about it, I never would have had the courage. But the time was right. It would be now or never.

"Sure," she answered right away, just in time for good old Brian to arrive.

"Sure what?" he asked.

"Sure is hot," Cathy said.

"What are you doing sitting in that hunk of junk?" he asked.

"Your car was locked and I didn't know where you hid the keys," Cathy answered with hostility.

She got up to follow him, as usual. I didn't want to push my luck. Besides, a Nova Scotia Parks truck had just pulled up and two real straight-looking guys in suits got out — real authority types.

One tall guy with a red tie just kind of stood there and eyed my car.

"Does this thing run or is it an abandoned vehicle?" he asked.

Brian, Belcher, and some of the foamheads were close enough to catch the drift. They were sucking it up. Sheer entertainment at my expense.

"Who owns this pile of scrap, anyway?" the other guy said looking right at me.

"It's mine," I said, trying to sound tough.

"Just wondering," the goon in the red tie said. He'd already done the damage. "You people mind explaining why you're loitering here?"

Now it was Brian's turn. "We're not loitering. We surf here. You have problems with that?" He did a much more convincing job of sounding tough and I could tell the two parks people didn't like the sound of him.

"Well, you should know, we've had some complaints ... garbage thrown around, noise, somebody driving up on the headland. We're planning on closing down this end of the beach. You'll have to park down there in the official parking lot and play it by our rules."

He pointed to the flat, bulldozed section of dusty gravel about a quarter mile away. I was remembering what Darlene had told me. Somehow I had hoped that she had got it wrong, and that the problem had just gone away. No such luck.

Suddenly I felt like one of the guys again. We all felt like we were about to get royally ripped off.

Belcher simply belched loudly. That was his trademark. He belched at anyone he didn't like.

"Why do you have to kick us out of here?" I asked.

"We have a development plan and it's been determined that everyone should park in the designated area."

"But we don't surf down there. We surf here."

"I guess you'll have to park there and walk."

"Why?" I asked.

"Because we have a plan," the guy in the red tie said. "What are you, deaf?"

Nobody knew quite what to say. One of the foam-heads with the open hatchback decided it was time to crank up his stereo full blast with his AC/DC tape.

The parks people just got back in their truck and gave me a disgusted look. They drove off back in the direction of the "designated parking area."

Brian turned on me now. "What is this crap, Randy. You live out here. Did you know about it?"

I should have said no, but I'm such lousy liar. "Well, yeah, sort of."

"Oh great," Brian said. "Well, why didn't you tell us about it? Maybe we could have done something."

"C'mon," he ordered Cathy, "let's get out of here."

Chapter Nine

Trouble at Rat Rock

I heard Kevin get out of bed and then he shook me hard on the shoulder. "It's five Rankle, let's go."

I was almost getting used to it. I kept telling myself it was worth it, that I was making good money and saving it up for something ... I didn't know what, but I'd use the money for something that would help me make sense out of my life.

Maybe all I needed was a decent car. Yeah, that was it. Improve the old image. Maybe buy some clothes. No, that was stupid. Why did I want to dress like a townie? Probably because that's what I really wanted to be. Even though I hated their guts.

That's the kind of stuff that ran through my head that morning.

"Move it, lard ass," Kevin hassled me, hauling the covers off and dragging me by the feet out of bed until I clunked on the floor.

I got dressed and looked outside. The dawn was cracking and I saw the dark clouds off towards sea. There was wind too. It was coming up out of the northeast.

That meant three things: a rough morning trip for fish, a raging storm and, after that, good waves. A northeaster meant a chance to ride the Big Left — a break at the headland at the eastern end of the beach which only broke on a northeast swell. Forget about the usual spot; it'd be nothing but chop for days but the Big Left would be cookin'. Even if the townies found their way out there and I didn't have it all to myself, they'd get mangled by the gnarly, unforgiving waves. And that would be a pleasure to watch.

It was a rough ride out Three Fathom Harbour and Kevin decided not to go down towards Lawrencetown at all. We'd stay close enough to the inlet so that if the wind came on fast and heavy, we could scoot for shore.

It was cold and ugly, even though it was mid-July. It goes that way along the shore here. Kev and I were hand-lining and pulling up good weight — mostly cod and hake, a few mackerel. I can't say I ever liked the work. This will sound a bit wacky but the whole time I was looking at squirming, dying fish I was thinking about Cathy. I figured that Brian had dumped on me and I didn't need to be loyal to him any more. And I had asked Cathy if she'd go out with me. She said yes.

"Then it's only a matter of actually asking her out," I said out loud to a ten-pound codfish, staring him straight in the old eyeball.

Kevin heard me above the rumble of the engine and the wind. "Rankle, you talking to fish now, buddy? I think we better take a break. Let's get some tea."

I threw the cod down into the bin and followed Kevin into the cabin.

Kevin put a pot on the propane cooker and we both stared into the blue flame. Now that I was inside, I could tell that the wind had actually come up quite a bit harder since we'd gone to sea.

"You gotta keep an eye on the ocean every minute," Kevin said.

"Swell's building. You won't be able to go out for a couple of days after this."

"There goes our good track record." We'd been to sea each morning now for twenty days straight. So much for my plan to only go out three days a week. At least now I'd have a chance for a small vacation.

"Means good waves. I'm looking forward to getting tubed at the Big Left."

"Big Left. Get off it. Randy, when are you gonna forget about that surfing bullshit? It's for kids. Grow up."

I knew there was no point in continuing the conversation. I looked out at the waves. The swells were up to maybe five feet, possibly six. Gulls dipped into the troughs and then shot like jets back up into the sky. By the time the real storm hit, they'd all be in the inlet or snug down on the water at Lawrencetown Lake.

Kevin pulled up the collar of his jacket and tucked his Moosehead cap down tight on his face. It was getting cold, even inside. We both felt cold and clammy with our rubber gear soaked with seawater .

"Kevin," I blurted out. "I want to ask a girl out and I don't quite know what to do. How do I do it? I mean, like what do I say?"

Kevin looked immediately very uncomfortable. He had that look that came over him like when he was singing in church. I knew he didn't have great luck with the ladies but he had taken out Rosalie Pettipas and Bev Lacey. I figured he must know something.

"Cripes, Randy. What do I look like, an expert? Shoot, I don't know. Just call her up and ask her if she wants to go park somewhere and drink some beer."

I could tell that this was going nowhere. Like I could really envision it. *Hi Cathy, it's Randy. Hey, I was wondering if you'd like to go park somewhere in my Chevette and maybe drink a case of Keith's. What do you think?*

No, I wasn't going to get much help from my brother. Kevin spit into the blue flame, as he often did when he didn't know what to say to me. He cranked off the gas, threw the rest of the tea from his cup onto the seawater on the floor. He opened the hatch door and we both looked out at the gale.

"Let's get the frig out of here," he said.

Kevin gunned the engine and we swung around and began punching the rolling sea as we pushed back towards shore. It was so noisy that it was impossible to talk. I hauled up the rest of the handlines while my brother held the wheel fast.

It seemed like a long, slow trip in. I wanted to sit down and get warm inside but knew that Kev would think I was a wimp, so I toughed it out, feeling the seawater that splashed over the hull drip down my neck until I shivered from the chill. We were just rounding Rat Rock when the engine began to sputter and it conked out. Kevin slammed his fist down hard on the cabin roof.

"Hold the goddamn wheel, Randy," he screamed at me.

"Got it," I said.

Kevin tore the lid off the engine bonnet and cursed again. "I knew it," he said, "The distributor cap's loose. It got wet. I'm gonna have to dry that sucker pretty quick."

"What'll we do?" I asked, trying not to sound worried. I could see that without the engine to pull us along we were drifting in closer and closer to the rocky shoal of Rat Rock.

"No sweat," Kevin said. He grabbed his tool box and whipped out a can of some spray stuff. I watched as he gave the distributer a healthy dose.

"Try her, buddy,"

I cranked the key but nothing happened.

Kevin wiped with a rag and then sprayed again. "Crank it, little brother, and do it right this time!" He knew it wasn't my fault that the damn thing wouldn't start. The engine cranked over but wouldn't fire.

We were about fifty feet now from a rock ledge. The choppy sea was pounding on it , sending up angry clouds of spray. The rocks were only maybe three feet under water. I didn't know whether I should say something and get my brother freaked out or just let him work.

Kevin was wrestling with the spray can and the distributor again. " Crank it now, Kevin," he yelled at me." And if you don't get it this time, I'm gonna heave your useless butt in the ocean."

I turned the key, bit my lip and said a little prayer. The rock ledge was just a few feet away from the hull.

It cranked and cranked but nothing. Then Kevin grabbed a hold of a spark plug wire he discovered that was loose and snapped it back onto the plug. He let out a loud curse as he received the full charge of the spark, taking a mean shock. But he got the wire in place. The engine sputtered, coughed, then roared into life.

I cranked on the wheel hard and pulled us straight back out to sea and deeper water.

Kevin fell over sideways, away from the engine and onto the deck. I aimed us as far away from the rock as I could, just in case the engine stalled again, then I cranked back around so we were aimed straight up the inlet towards the wharf on Causeway Road.

When Kevin got to his feet, I could tell that he was really shook up. I guess he knew how close we were to Rat Rock and how close we were to losing the boat.

"Next time we might have to swim home," I said, trying to sound nonchalant.

Kevin was rubbing his hand where he had taken the massive shock from the alternator as the engine kicked over. "Maybe you'll have to swim home, little brother. Not me."

He said it like it was some sort of insult thrown back in my face, his way of trying to cover up that he was scared to death. But I knew there was a certain amount of truth in it. My stubborn brother, for all his great abilities, had never learned to swim a stroke in his entire life.

Chapter Ten

A Monumental Night

I think it was the close call we had with Rat Rock that gave me the courage to get on the phone to Cathy. I knew her last name was Evans but I had never asked her for a phone number, which shows you how much I know about arranging these things. But if I could face down a shipwreck on the rocks without losing my guts, then I figured I could at least handle this. So I started calling every Evans in the Halifax phone book. I said, " Hi, is Cathy there?" and waited to see if I had the right house. I even got another Cathy Evans — a seventy-year-old lady — but eventually I found the right one. It turned out she lived on Oxford Street in the south end of Halifax.

"You said you might consider going out with me," I said.

"Sure."

"Well, how about tonight?"

"Okay," she said. So far so good.

"So what would you like to do?" I knew I couldn't suggest Kevin's idea.

"Whatever you want."

Well this conjured up one wonderful fantasy but I wasn't going to suggest *that*. "Well what do you usually do when you go out?" I almost said, "when you go out with Brian," but I couldn't bring myself to say it. I didn't even want to think about that turkey.

"Sometimes we just go to the Park Lane. You know, go in the shops, hang out by the waterfall or see a movie."

That was it. "We'll go see a movie. I'll pick you up at seven."

It was a monumental night of my life. Things went without a hitch. I picked her up and we went to this fancy shopping mall on Spring Garden Road. When we got to the movies inside, it turned out there were six theatres. Shoot, I had just figured we'd see whatever was on. Now I had to make a decision. Playing was the latest Rambo sequel, an Eddie Murphy film, a Ninja flick, and a film about a bear. I picked the one about the bear.

Cathy thought my selection was really weird ... "but cute," she said. "Brian would have picked Stallone or the Ninja stuff. Only you would pick the bear movie." I think it was because I always identified with bears. Maybe it was because I was built like one. Anyway, the film was okay. There was lots of good scenery and stuff and not a bad story. I put my arm around Cathy but I didn't put any moves on. I was afraid my luck wouldn't hold.

Afterwards, we sat down by a green waterfall inside the mall and we talked.

"I got thinking about the beach again," Cathy said, "thinking about what we talked about ... you know, how things were changing and getting messed up. So I made a few phone calls?"

"You did? Who'd you call?"

"I talked to the deputy minister of the parks department."

Once again Cathy was full of surprises. The girl had guts. "What did you say to him?"

"I told him there were two kinds of endangered species at the beach: the plovers and the surfers. I explained the situation and asked him if he'd look into it."

"What'd he say?" I couldn't imagine that a big shot in government would pay any attention to a teenage girl who calls up on the phone.

"He promised he would and I insisted that he get back to me within a week. I promised to send him some information I photocopied about both the bird and about surfing."

"You're too much," I said and then I guess I kind of lost my concentration so I just sat there with a goofy look on my face. I couldn't think of anything else to say and she finally asked me if anything interesting had happened to me today.

I told her about the near disaster from the morning. She looked really concerned. "It sounds dangerous."

"It was," I said and I told her about Kevin trying to get the engine going.

"Tell me about your family."

At first I was afraid to get into it but she seemed interested so I told her about my fisherman brother, my welder father and about my mom who mostly just cooks and washes clothes and takes care of us and, oh yeah, goes to bingo three nights a week.

"Boy, that's different," Cathy said. "It sounds really ... really neat." But I could tell she was at a loss for words.

"So what's your old man do?" I asked.

"He's vice president of an investment company. And my mom runs an advertising agency."

"That's cool," I said, but I could tell that this little conversation had just opened up a big canyon between us. Cathy pulled a loonie out of her purse and heaved it into the pool. I was pretty freaked. The girl had just thrown away a whole dollar for nothing.

"Why'd you do that?"

"It's for luck," she said. "Yours. I want it all to be good." Next, she gave me a little kiss on the cheek and stood up. It meant it was time to take her home.

"Tell me about Brian," I said as I drove her home. I needed to know if she was really serious with him. I wanted to know if I had a chance.

"What's there to tell?" She wanted to avoid the subject.

"Do you love him?" I blurted out, gripping hard on the steering wheel.

She wasn't going to give me a straight answer. "He can be a real jerk sometimes. As you well know. Sometimes I think that what he needs is for someone to show him that he can't always be at the top. He needs to be brought back down to reality. I keep expecting someone to straighten him out. But no one has done it yet." She took a deep breath. "Brian and I have been together a long time. We're good for each other. I just wish he'd stop ordering me around."

"So why don't you dump him?"

"Maybe I will some day."

We stopped in front of her house. I got out to walk her up to her door, but she touched my hand. "That's okay. Stay there. See you around." She was sounding rather formal now. "One more thing. Don't tell Brian. Okay?"

Chapter Eleven

The Big Left

The next day, it was pretty easy to talk Kevin out of going out on the boat. The wind was still up out of the northeast. It wasn't raining but the day looked pretty grim. I drove over to the beach and saw that the waves were blown out, big and sloppy, but when I pulled up by the headland at the other end of the beach I could see that I had been right about one thing: the Big Left was big and mean and wrapping left around the point with ferocious power. The northeaster had really jacked up a swell. I never went surfing there by myself. It was a dangerous place. If you got nailed by a wave, it slammed you with a heavy, thick wallop and then dragged you in close to the rocks in a savage current that wouldn't let up until you'd been bounced off the boulders in a heavy shorebreak.

The only times I'd been out there was with Reggie and Chris. They taught me respect for the place. I thought about just going back home and getting some extra sleep to make up for all the early mornings I'd been keeping. I still had this glow on from my night with Cathy.

And then I had this idea. Cathy had said that Brian needed to be put in his place, right? And who better to do that than me. I mean, look at the way he treated me the other day ... like I was part of a conspiracy with the parks people. So I decided to give Brian a call.

"Brian, it's Randy. I thought you might want a wave report."

"Randy?" He sounded pretty surprised. "You mean there's rideable waves today at the beach. I thought it was the middle of a storm. I called the weather office. They said northeast winds for the next two days."

"So?" I was toying with him.

"So the beach will be blown out with chop."

"Yeah, but the Big Left is rippin'."

"I've never surfed the Big Left. I never saw it break."

"Well, it's breaking now. The wind is offshore there. Conditions are perfect. I was looking for some company. You up for it?"

"Sure." Brian couldn't back down now. I had him in a vice lock.

"It's not like the point at the Beach. You're sure you're ready for it?"

"Are you kidding?"

"Okay, but look, don't get Belcher or Fitz. I don't think they're ready for it."

"Maybe you're right. Meet you there in an hour. This should be a blast."

Already I felt guilty. I'd seen people get pummelled at the Big Left. It looked easy but if you were a split second off, it would have your face.

It was drizzling by the time I got to the Big Left. Brian showed up right on time. He parked up high off the road where the old railroad tracks had been. The windows of his car were all steamed up and I didn't think anybody was with him, but when he opened the door I saw Cathy sitting there. My heart sank down to my knees.

But what the heck. She'd be able to sit there and watch. Maybe that was the way it should be. In a way, this was her idea.

I saw Brian say something to her, then get out. He already had his gear on. "She's just gonna watch today. I brought along some binoculars so she wouldn't have to go outside and get her hair wet." He said it like it was some sort of inside joke. Cathy gave me a smile but then closed the door right away and didn't even say hi. I think she was afraid I might say something about last night.

I led Brian on the long walk out to the point. The wind was raging so hard it was tough just to hang onto our boards as we walked.

"That board is kind of short for this sort of break," I told him.

Now it was the old Brian. "I'd rather be on this than that old stick of yours."

"Whatever you say. Just be careful, okay?" And with that I ran down the rocks and threw my board into the white foaming water. I knew Brian would follow. I was headed right into the worst place to paddle out and Brian fell for it. He followed me right out toward the churning whitewater. I turned turtle and let it wash over me, then I scrambled like mad to paddle back into the deep so I could sneak past the next cracking wave. But Big Brian didn't know about turning turtle in heavy soup. I couldn't help but crack a smile as I saw him get twisted around and pushed under.

He was washed in nearly as far as the cars before he could get his bearings and begin a long paddle back out to sea in the deeper trench. To tell you the truth, I really hoped that he would quit then and there. He had already taken a pounding that would have made me think twice about going back for more punishment. But Brian wasn't a guy who took defeat lightly.

The waves were maybe seven feet. That was pretty big by local standards. The northeast wind was slightly offshore from where I sat and that was making the lip of the wave throw way out before it came crashing down. Like I said, it was a completely different wave from the ones any of us were used to surfing.

The water was brown and murky from rain running down the dirt cliff of the headland that stared you straight in the face as you sat, waiting to catch a wave. The wind also wanted to blow you out to sea so you had to keep paddling into it just to stay in place. This was nobody's idea of a good time, just survival surfing. But it was my chance to show Brian that he hadn't learned as much as he thought, and he needed that lesson.

I saw Brian still struggling to get out of the deep water and closer to the line-up of the break. I knew the current and knew that he was having a real struggle but I also knew he wouldn't quit.

I waited for a monster close-out set to pass by me, and then I paddled for a relatively sane looking five-footer. I thought it would be an easy wave and that I was near the shoulder but no sooner was I making the drop than it jacked up behind me and loomed overhead. I could see a thick heavy brown lip of water shoot over my hair. I ducked down, pulled a rail hard into the wave and tried to ride it high, only to get caught by the wave and slammed over the falls and down to the bottom. I dove deep with it and let it sweep past me like a steam roller.

When I came back up for air, I felt cold and shaken. Maybe old Brian was about to get the best of me. I felt that I was about to get caught in that killer current along the rocks and I had to tow my board by my leash and dive under two oncoming waves to get out of its grip.

I paddled back to Brian, winded and weary.

"I made a mistake, Brian," I said. "I shouldn't have brought you out here. They are much meaner than they look. Let's just forget it. We'll paddle up the beach and catch the shorebreak in."

I meant every word of it. I knew when I was in over my head. But Brian had got his wind back. He was smiling. "No way, Randy. Just 'cause that wave had you for lunch doesn't mean I can't handle it."

He paddled for a wave, but the wind pushed him backwards off the top before he could get down it. As the wave broke, and the wind blew back the spray, we both got showered by bitter cold seawater.

Brian kept trying to catch waves but he wasn't in the right spot. The wind kept killing his speed and he couldn't get down the face of a wave on take-off. Maybe he'd eventually give up. I wouldn't give him a word of advice. Maybe he simply wouldn't catch a damn thing and that would be embarrassing enough. I'd be satisfied.

I saw a set coming our way and decided to try again. If nothing else, I'd take a smaller wave in and that might lure Brian back onto the shore.

This time I was a split second ahead of the freight train. I dropped down the face, made my turn, began to race across a long, brown wave. It was as steep as the side of a building and looked like it wanted nothing better than to collapse on top of me. I sped way down the line, then kicked out just as it closed over onto the rocks.

I paddled to shore and sat down panting on some rocks. *C'mon Brian, go for a little teaser, then paddle in.* No such luck. I watched as he struggled to catch wave after wave. The wind blew him back each time.

Damn. I paddled back out. I didn't like leaving him out there alone and if I stayed on shore, he'd probably think I had turned chicken.

"Just taking a little break," I said when I got back to the line-up.

Brian ignored me and now paddled further inside and closer to the point. "Forget it!" I yelled. "If a big set comes you'll get nailed. You're too far inside."

But, of course, he ignored me. He tried for another pair of waves and still couldn't get up. Then I saw the dark humps on the horizon. I pointed out to sea and tried to wave him back my way, into the deep water. Instead, he stayed put.

Like an idiot, he went for the first wave. That meant that if he got creamed, there'd be at least five more right after it to clean up the body parts.

"No!" I yelled. But it was too late.

It was like slow motion. Brian was digging hard, not paying attention to what was going on. Then, the wave had him. He was pushing himself up from his board but he was already inside the elevator shaft. It was just straight down. I saw the nose of his board bite in deep, then I watched from the side as Brian took it chin first into the trough. As the wave passed by me, I could see arms, legs and board, all wrapped together and being sucked up the back of the wave, then over the falls in that thick heavy brown water.

I cringed at the thought, knowing exactly what it would feel like. Suddenly there was a wave right on top of me. I was about to get what Brian had just experienced. Instinct took over and I grabbed the nose of my board and punched through the steep wall, heading straight for sea. I let one, two, three waves go by, all too critical to take off on. From the top of one of the swells, I looked for Brian. Damn. I saw his board, busted in half, crashing up on the rocks. No Brian.

Then I saw him. All three waves had dumped on him with all the vengeance of an uncaring North Atlantic. He was getting in close to the rocks and I knew that it would be new to him.

He wouldn't know how to stay in the deep part of the water until the waves passed. He'd try to pull himself up on the shore now that he'd lost his board, and that would be worse.

One wave left in the set. I was almost too late for it, but I had to get in there. As I pushed off down the face, I looked up and I saw Brian's car in by the railway tracks. I saw the door open and Cathy get out. She was running towards the shore.

I raced for the shoulder of the wave, felt myself get pulled back inch by inch into the mangling tunnel that should have been the biggest thrill of the summer. But all I felt was fear. If I screwed up, I'd never get to Brian. I felt myself assaulted from all sides — the wave, the chop up the face of the wave, the wind — but I hung on like I was glued to my stick.

I shot out of the tunnel in a puff of air and saw that I was within feet of Brian. He was flopping his arms around, just trying to keep his head up when the whitewater from my wave caught him and pulled him back under.

Next, I watched as it lifted him up and hammered him down close to the rocky shore. I turned around and saw another monster set coming our way. There would be no let up. I had maybe a full minute before the next wave would be on us. My arms seemed to work on their own. I paddled to Brian and got him to heave himself up on my board. Then I aimed us straight back to sea.

"Where the hell are you going?" he screamed at me in a hoarse croak.

"Just hang on and paddle."

He was laying down near the nose and I had to flop down on top of him so I could get us headed out to sea and paddle. It was like pulling dead weight.

Man, I had never been so winded in my life. But I finally convinced him we had to go out, not in. And he started to paddle when we were faced with the prospect of going over backwards down the face of an incoming massive wall of water.

I didn't say a thing more. I could see Cathy now on the shoreline, running, waving her arms and pointing to precisely the only safe place to get ashore. I think the girl instinctively understood things about the ocean.

It took twenty more minutes of paddling against wind and current to get us out of the danger zone and into a safe place to get out of the water. I heaved my board down and lay out flat on the rocks.

Cathy ran over and she was helping Brian further up the shore.

After I got my wind back, I walked over to the two of them. "Anything broken?" I asked.

"Only my board." Brian said. He sounded defeated. "Screw it. Anyway, thanks." I know that was a hard thing for him to say. If I hadn't dragged him back outside I know he would have done some real damage. Maybe he would have broken his back and drowned. Maybe I should have felt like a hero but I felt like a creep.

When Cathy finally looked up at me and said nothing, I felt worse than that. I felt like I had become the lowest form of living scum on the planet earth.

Chapter Twelve

Big Waves and Tube Rides

The weather hung on for three more days so there was no fishing, and for me, no surfing. What I did was sleep. Sleep had always been my favourite form of escape. When I wasn't asleep, I watched TV — you know, game shows, dumb comedies. I even sat through a couple of my mom's soap operas which was pretty bizarre because she kept explaining to me what had happened to all the characters before. She talked about them like they were all close friends.

Sure, I kept up a watch on the waves. I wasn't going back to the Big Left, not by myself, and I wasn't going to drag any other sucker out there.

Kevin put some new wires and a distributor cap on his boat motor and my old man welded the frame of Linc Wynacht's ancient white Cadillac. Linc didn't have a red cent to pay my old man, so he said my dad might as well keep the car. It was over twenty years old and Linc had decided he was only throwing good money after bad.

I tried getting Cathy on the phone but whoever answered just kept saying she wasn't there. I even tried calling Brian to apologize about getting him into trouble at the Left but as soon as I started talking, he hung up on me. He didn't even give a darn that I had probably saved his life. So now I had lost Cathy and had made an enemy of Brian. Great.

When the weather cleared, I put in my morning's work on the boat and then drove over to the beach. The side of the road was jam packed with more foam-heads than I'd ever seen. I think somebody in Halifax must have been giving away boogie boards. And there were about twelve surfers in the line-up at the point. Jeez, I'd never seen it so crowded. The waves were still choppy and not so great looking.

I saw Brian's car and I saw Cathy sitting alone on the rocks.

"Hi Cathy," I said, trying to sound humble.

"That was really stupid, you know. What were you trying to prove?" she exploded, like a volcano waiting all this time to go off.

"I made a mistake," I said. "I thought he could handle it."

"No you didn't. You took him out there on purpose because you wanted to see him get ripped apart by those waves." I had never seen a girl so angry before. It was pretty scary.

"I didn't exactly make him do it."

"You knew what Brian was like. You knew he wouldn't back down."

"Yeah, but you said he needed somebody to show him he couldn't always be the top dog. Right?"

"Is that why you did it? Randy, I sure figured you wrong. I just didn't think you were so crude."

I think *crude* was the word that dug in like a knife. It described perfectly what I'd always felt about myself. *Crude*. So crude that Cathy would probably never want to talk to me again. Suddenly I felt real disgusted again with who I was. I looked out at all the townies having fun in the waves ... like they were one big happy family. Now that I was on the outside again, I wanted, more than anything in the world, to be part of that family. I didn't care what it took.

I grabbed my board and paddled out. First, I stayed inside with the boogie boarders. A lot of them were new kids, only thirteen or fourteen, who didn't have the slightest idea of what to do with a wave. I started introducing myself and giving advice. When I took a few quick little close-out waves and kicked myself right up into the sky as the wave collapsed, they could see that I knew what I was talking about.

They didn't say much except stuff like, "Hey dude, all right," every time I got a good ride, but that was enough.

Later, I paddled out to the point. Brian kept a clear distance from me. So did Fitz and Belcher. I wondered if they knew about the Big Left. "You guys should try the Big Left like me and Brian some time," I said to them, but they didn't say anything. Brian just gave me a kind of sick look.

Over the next few days I got to know some of the new guys — Hobbs and Tony and Doobs. It was like the beginning of the summer again. They thought I was cool because I knew more about surfing than they did and because I could thrash waves better than anyone.

On the beach, though, it was a different scene. Brian still ruled the side of the road. He had a way of just leaning on his car in his shades and jams and surf shirts. I heard him talking bull about big waves and tube rides and the young guys were sucking it up. So was Cathy, it looked like, who wouldn't give me the time of day any more.

Everyone was pretty rowdy with loud music, wet-suits tossed all over the place and guys changing right down to bare-ass on the side of the road. You could tell that really grossed-out family types driving down the Shore with station-wagons full of little kids.

Every once in a while, those two parks guys would drive by, slow down, and just sort of take it all in with disgust until Brian or someone gave them the finger. I knew where all of this was headed and I wanted to say something but I knew that I'd just get shot down. They'd think I was a wimp.

Chapter Thirteen

My New Image

Even though I was beginning to hate Brian again ... and everything he stood for ... I wanted to be just like him. I felt cheated that I didn't grow up in the south end of Halifax and that I didn't have money to spend on clothes and cars and gear. I decided it was my parents' fault and that it wasn't fair to me at all. So I figured that I would, in my own way, try to do something about it.

"What are you gonna do with Whynacht's Caddie?" I asked my old man.

"I'd take fifty dollars from the first customer who was fool enough to offer it," he said.

I went into my room and counted out five tens, carried them to the kitchen and threw them down on the table where my father was drinking black tea.

"You'll never be able to keep that contraption in gas and oil," he said.

"Yes I will," I answered.

And so began my new image. As soon as I had it licensed, I drove in to Park Lane Shopping Mall, paid to park it in the underground garage and blew two hundred bucks on clothes. I paid over fifty dollars for a pair of sunglasses that I thought made me look like

Tom Cruise. So what if my gut still stuck out? I was convinced the new image would make a world of difference.

By the time I got home from that trip, I had burned about twenty dollars worth of gas. Add to that five bucks for parking and two hundred big ones for clothes and it was starting to add up to a very expensive lifestyle. And here's the clincher. I had to walk past the only surf shop in town. They had a dynamite board on sale. So I bought it. Then the cute girl behind the counter talked me into buying a flashy wetsuit as well. But why worry? I was making good money from fishing.

And then to celebrate, I picked up a couple of cases of beer from the liquor commission. Old Gulf Minot out at the wharf had told me it was okay with him if I used his fishing shack on Causeway Road for a party, as long as we didn't burn it down. It was near sundown when I invited all the guys and a few girls from the beach out to party with me. Everyone was really freaked by the white Caddie and maybe my new duds too but I think the thing that got them the most was the beer in the back seat.

Confident now that I had made a serious impression, I walked over and asked Cathy if she wanted to come too. She just shook her head and smiled. "I don't know. Maybe I'll come later," she said.

But she never showed up. Instead, the foamheads and the other new surfers came and drank up all my beer.

The other fishermen on Causeway Road were pretty annoyed by all the noise but nobody hassled us.

"What is this, like a condominium or something?" Tony asked. "I've never seen a place like this before."

"No, man," Hobbs said. "This is like a time warp. Look at this place. We have just stepped back one hundred years into the past."

The townies got a big laugh out of the fishing shack and after a while went out running around on the wharf until Darrel Bellefountaine got right angry. He said he'd call the cops if they didn't stop messing around with the nets and traps on the wharf.

The beer didn't go too far and Tony said something about everybody going back to his house in Halifax, that his folks were gone on a business trip.

"C'mon, dude," he said to me, "you too. Let's get back in the time machine and travel to the twentieth century."

"I'll pass," I said. It was funny because up to that minute I had been having a really good time. It was my first party and everything had been going great. "Be careful," I told them, suddenly feeling guilty that even though nobody could have had more than a couple of bottles of Moosehead, it might be enough to get somebody in trouble if he wasn't used to drinking beer. I should have said more, but it was like a wind had swept through the old shack and cleaned everybody out. I heard the cars chase off down the gravel road and I was left alone, sitting by a kerosene lamp feeling hollow inside. I had this image in my head of a cod after Kevin had slit his belly, scooped out all his guts with a knife and then thrown it on the dock.

Chapter Fourteen

Liberate the Beach

I don't think Kevin knew what was going on when I started waking *him* up at four-thirty instead of five-thirty.

"Rankle, what's come over you?"

"Money, big brother. Lots of it. I need money. My car needs money. My lifestyle needs money."

"Lifestyle. What kind of talk is that?"

"Come on, Kev. If we get out an hour early, we catch more fish. I make more money, you make more money. We're all happy, right?"

"Can't argue with that logic," he said, getting out of bed and wincing as his bare feet touched the cold linoleum floor. I made some bologna sandwiches and we were out into the early morning gloom, into the boat and headed past Rat Rock before the sun was up.

The beach scene was getting a little tense. The surfers and foamheads hung out along the road by the rocks and on the beach. The parks people hated it. We knew something was coming and we had been warned.

Then one day, I drove up early in the afternoon, not wanting any hassles, just a few clean summer waves, a chat with the guys and then home for a nap. But the roadway was all jammed up.

There was a backhoe and a dumptruck and a bunch of highways workers putting in massive wooden posts for a guard rail. Already there were about twenty "No Parking" signs on metal posts.

I left my Caddie by the side of the road and walked up to the old hang-out in disbelief.

Fitz was shaking his fist at the foreman and calling him a fascist pig.

I saw Brian trying to talk some of the workmen out of putting in the posts. But most of the guys were just standing around yelling at the workmen. They said things like, "You can't keep us out of here," and "Liberate Lawrencetown Beach!" and stuff like that.

I saw the two parks officials from before standing with their arms folded up on the headland and I hiked up to them.

"Why are you doing this?" I asked. "Where are we supposed to park?"

"We told you," the creep who always wore the red tie said, "down in the designated parking area."

"That sucks," I answered. I was boiling mad.

"Doesn't matter. It's the way it is."

"What can we do to change the way it is?" I asked.

"Nothing," he told me. "We have a plan and the plan calls for a boardwalk along here and no parking."

"People will ignore the signs. Everyone, including tourists, will be stopping their cars on the road and you'll end up with accidents. People getting killed."

"Kid, give us a break. We got a plan for this park and surfers just aren't in it. We've done studies of the land-use here ... and the traffic flow too. It's been determined that you already cause problems with traffic flow around the corner there."

"Yeah, but this will just make it worse."

And then our attention was caught by the fact that Belcher and Fitz had decided to go into combat with one of the guard posts already put into the ground. They were kicking it back and forth with karate kicks until it loosened itself. Next, I watched as Brian picked the massive six-foot post up out of the ground and, struggling through the traffic, threw it in the ditch on the other side of the road.

"That does it," the other parks guy said. "I'm calling the police."

I hiked back down the hill and watched as the some of the guys went about the work of twisting "No Parking" signs off their metal sticks and pulling up four other posts. The scene was really getting intense.

Tony yelled at me to come help him haul out the post he was working on but I pretended I didn't hear him. The workmen started yelling at the surfers and I saw one guy pick up a shovel and swing at Brian. Brian grabbed the shovel and yanked it away from the worker. I thought he was about to whack him over the head but instead he just threw it over the rocks onto the beach.

The parks officials walked past me towards their truck. I could see the guy in the red tie talking into his two-way radio. He had the Cole Harbour RCMP station and asked them to send somebody out.

Then he looked me hard in the eye and said, "I hope you know we're willing to prosecute."

I guess he thought I was the brains behind this.

"Shove it buddy!" Doobs screamed to him at the top of his lungs.

"Liberate Lawrencetown Beach!" Belcher yelled and heaved another post off the road. Cars were blowing their horns and some of the guys began to pound on their hoods.

I looked around for Cathy and saw her sitting in Brian's car with the windows rolled up. She looked good and scared. I'm sure she figured somebody was going to get hurt.

I walked over to her and knocked on the window. The car was half on the road and blocking traffic.

"Are you all right?" I asked.

Just then the Mountie cruiser came over the crest of the hill. Seeing the jam-up ahead, the driver put on the siren and flashed the red lights.

A few cars parted and let the police car through. When it pulled to a stop, I saw that it was Darlene. She spoke something into her radio and then opened the door, stood outside and put on her hat.

She had a night stick in her hand and looked tough as nails.

"All right, what's going on here?"

The two parks people started towards her but all the guys started yelling foul things at them.

Darlene picked up her radio phone and flicked on the outside horn. "Okay, everybody just calm down," she said. The guys stopped yelling. Darlene looked around trying to size up the situation. Over her radio came a raspy message from headquarters. "Do you need back-up? Repeat, do you need back-up?"

She paused for a minute, flicked the handset back to radio and said, "Negative, Cole Harbour."

And at that minute, I felt kind of proud of my old cousin who was ready to sort out this mob scene single-handed.

She was back on the horn. "I want anyone who has a car parked illegally on the pavement to get in it and drive off. Now."

The guy in the tie immediately began to protest. "They're responsible for wanton destruction!" he snarled through his teeth but Darlene motioned him away with her night stick.

"That's it. Take it slow and move off down the road. We gotta let this traffic through."

The highways workers grumbled but a few of them laughed. The parks people were boiling mad.

Darlene was scanning the crowd, completely cool. Surfers were starting to drive away. The mob was thinning. Then Darlene saw me. Her face was one big question mark. But I didn't give her eye contact. I looked away. I didn't want to get involved.

All but Fitz, Belcher and Brian had simply gotten in their cars and driven off, satisfied, I reckoned, that they weren't going to get arrested.

Darlene listened to what the parks officials and the highway foreman had to say. They seemed pretty ticked-off that she had let everyone go.

Afterwards, she walked over to me. Brian was talking to Cathy. Belcher and Fitz were sitting on the hood of his car.

"What's this all about, Randy?" she asked. I wished that she hadn't used my name. I didn't want anyone to know that I had a Mountie for cousin or a friend.

"I don't know a thing about it," I said in a cold, hard voice, pretending she was a complete stranger.

I could tell by her expression that she was hurt.

"Okay. We'll talk later, Rankle," she said. Turning to Brian she said, "You wanna move this vehicle out of the traffic before I give you a ticket?"

"Yes, ma'am," Brian answered, faking politeness. "Right away, constable."

As she moved on to hassle someone else, Brian turned to me. *"Rankle?* Is that like a pet name or something?" And he got in his car and fired it up.

"How come you didn't invite *her* to your party, boy scout?" Fitz asked me.

Chapter Fifteen

Hurricane Donna

I was just about to fall asleep when I heard a car pull up my driveway and a knock at the door. I heard a low voice and then my mom was yelling to me upstairs.

"Randy, get down here. It's Darlene. She wants to see you."

I threw on my clothes and walked downstairs. Darlene looked right fired-up about something.

"Sit down," she said. I sat down at the kitchen table.

"What the hell was that today, anyway?"

I shrugged. How did I begin to explain?

"You know, if I wanted to, I could have put you all in jail. And I probably should have. Vandalism. Public nuisance and obscenity. Take your pick!"

"Look, I wasn't the one knocking out the posts. I tried to talk the parks folks out of putting them in, that's all. I tried to be reasonable." But there was something else bothering Darlene. It wasn't just the obnoxious surfers.

"Yeah, well was it reasonable when you pretended that you didn't even know who I was?"

She was right. I didn't want the other guys to think that I knew her.

"It's kind of complicated. I'm, sorry."

Darlene grabbed my arm, gave it hard twist and held it that way. That was just like what she'd do when we were kids and we'd get into some stupid argument about who was a better hockey player, Wayne Gretzsky or Bobby Orr. But now she was stronger. It hurt.

"You're breaking my arm," I said, sounding like a little brat who had just lost a fight.

Darlene let go. "I should break your head. I thought we were friends. I thought at least you wouldn't let my job get between us. It wasn't like I was asking you to rat on your buddies. All I wanted out there from you today was for you to acknowledge me. You could have said, 'I'm, sorry Darlene, I don't know what's going on' ... but instead you acted like I had just arrived from another planet."

"I'm sorry."

"That's not enough. I'm gonna stay mad at you until you figure out some decent way to apologize."

I didn't know how. She got up to go. "Look, cuz, while you're hard at figuring out how to apologize, you better tell your buddies to be careful. It seems you got the highways crew refusing to go back and put in the guard rail until this thing is straightened out. The parks people are having a fit. I expect you'll have the park guards harassing you at every chance they can, but as long as you're parked along the road, it's highways' right-of-way and not their jurisdiction. I think you're all getting a rotten deal ... but smarten up. Negotiate with the parks people. Right now you have all enemies and no allies. I'm on your side, remember ... or at least I was."

She closed the door hard behind her. I didn't quite know how to read that last statement. Enemies and allies. Yeah, I counted up my enemies: the parks dudes, Brian, Cathy, Darlene, probably most of the townies. Pretty soon all I'd have left on my side was me.

Just then Kevin walked into the kitchen, opened the fridge and cracked open a can of Pepsi.

"What was all that about?" he asked. "Sounded like World War Three out here."

"Darlene's pissed off at me."

"I thought she still had a crush on you."

"Get off it."

"Then what were the fireworks for?"

I explained about the battle at the beach.

"You and your surf kooks take that whole thing pretty seriously. I don't get it. What's so great about dangling your toes off of a floating piece of plastic into cold seawater?"

"You should try it. Though you'd have to learn to swim first."

"Yeah, I'd have to learn to swim," said Kevin sarcastically. "Anyway, I get enough salt water in a day to keep me happy. Let's get to bed so we don't feel like dead doorknobs at five-thirty tomorrow."

"Four-thirty," I said. "We missed a lot of days and better catch up. I need the money."

"You know, you're the only fisherman I know who drives a Cadillac. That's real class."

He was goofing on me, but it felt good. Ever since we did battle with Rat Rock, Kevin had treated me less like a fat little brother and more like a human being. But before I had a chance to get up from the kitchen table, Kevin put his thumb over the pop can, shook hard and let me have a blast of Pepsi that shot straight up my nose.

By the time the last half of August rolled around, I had put in enough days of fishing to last me a lifetime. I suggested to Kevin we lay low for a while. But Kevin said it was the best summer he ever had and we'd have to quit soon enough when fall rolled around.

But the first really big hurricane of the season, Donna, came heading up the Eastern Seaboard. That mean two things: rough seas and, sooner or later, righteous waves.

I studied the news and the weather maps. Donna tore across Puerto Rico killing nearly a hundred people, and laying waste to villages, leaving people homeless. I should have felt sorry for them, but I just kept thinking about the powerhouse waves soon to come our way if the storm tracked up the coastline.

And it did. Donna flooded the Carolina coast and went a bit further out to wreak havoc on Bermuda. It kept pulling north and then it began to stall. On the weather map, there was this huge spiralling mass of low pressure sitting a few hundred miles off Sable Island. Usually a storm like that would just keep going further out to sea until it died a quiet death in the cold northern waters but this one was different.

I woke up in the middle of a dead quiet night on August the eighteenth to the deep booming sound of a major groundswell at sea. I got up in the dark and drove my Caddie over to the headland, right up to the edge of the drop-off so I could shine my headlights out to sea. At first I saw the dense walls of whitewater, and then, as I hit the high beams, further out I could see walls of water, maybe eight feet high. The air felt warm and full of life. I knew something exciting was about to happen.

The next morning Kevin woke me to go out on the boat. I told him about the waves and he wouldn't believe me. But as soon as we got the boat fired up and headed out the inlet, he got the point. We watched as Giff DeLong tried to push out through the powerful swells driving up the inlet until he nearly swamped. The waves weren't steep or critical, just big and fat and very different from the local chop and easy rollers that usually found their way up the inlet.

Kevin was at the wheel and I didn't say anything as he took his usual route out, near the shore and not in the deep channel where we should have been. He called it his short cut. But I could see that we were too close to shore. And we were running nearly sideways to a deep rolling swell that was about to jack up on the shallows. We took a heavy jarring as Kevin tried to change direction but not quick enough.

Kev looked a little surprised. "Let's go back in. This isn't worth it," I said.

But we were in the trough between two seven-foot swells and Kevin was just plain stubborn.

"They're only waves, Rankle. Don't chicken out on me yet."

But I could see that Kevin had it all wrong. We were sideways to the swell again and the only way we would keep from dumping was if we went straight into it and took the brunt of it on the bow.

"You idiot!" I yelled at him. "Go straight into it!"

Kevin looked at me like I had just said something stupid.

Too late. The wave washed in partly over the side and splashed a gusher of water all across the boat. I grabbed onto something to stay upright and then decided to get serious.

"Let me do it!" I said, grabbing the wheel away from my brother. He seemed a bit dazed from the minor swamping and for the first time in his life thought that maybe I had more sense than he did.

Another swell was headed our way, not bigger but the same as the others. I wanted deep water and I wanted it fast, but first I had to take my own advice. I gunned the engine and shot her straight up the face of the wave. I could feel it through my boots as the bow kissed air and the engine roared as half the boat lifted up out of the sea. It was a heavy old crate and I was trusting that the dead weight would keep us from pitch-poling over backwards. I was right.

Then I ran her for the deepest part of the channel and aimed straight back in for the wharf. Not another wave had a chance to wrestle with us.

"Time for a little vacation, bro," I said, throwing a line onto the dock. I jumped off and ran for my car. Even Kevin would be convinced now that it wouldn't be worth fishing for a few days.

Chapter Sixteen

Beachbreak Bozo

That afternoon, the beach was mobbed with tourists, sunbathers and swimmers. It was completely unlike Nova Scotia. The sun was out and the air was hot. A light breeze from the land blew a warm, near-tropical breeze on the place. The water was as warm as it ever gets and the lifeguards along the main stretch of the beach had their hands full.

A great, growling shorebreak lifted swimmers high in the air and slammed them down right along the sand, then shoved them well up on the beach before retreating back to sea in a scraping groan as rocks and pebbles rattled back down into the deep trench.

But the shorebreak was nothing compared to the long, green walls of water breaking further out on the sandbar. These were truly tropical waves, hurricane waves. We were getting the big waves from the storm further out but, luckily, not the lousy weather. Here, the sun was out and the wind was a warm easy land breeze that helped to stand the waves straight up and down.

Cars were parked along both sides of the road by the headland and as far as the eye could see down the

beach. The official parking lot was already overflow-
ing. The planners had failed to plan for this. Word
about the big waves and warm water had spread and
the place was crawling with people.

I had to park my Caddie half in a ditch but I didn't
care. I wanted those waves. I grabbed my board, gave
it a quick waxing and ran like a madman for the
water. The sea was littered with boogie boarders and
surfers. Where'd they all come from? But as I looked
around I could see that these were mostly kids who
were new to it. They were getting rattled by the six
and seven-foot waves. There were plenty of late take-
offs with major pearl-diving straight to the bottom.
But heck, the water was warm. As long as one could
swim and stay out of the rip current, no one should
get hurt.

I paddled out first to the sandbar break and check-
ed out the scene. Ratty looking little kids with new
boogie boards and Churchill fins were clawing to drop
in on the waves. I found Tony and Doobs on their
surfboards and watched as they got plastered by a
clean-up set that rolled through at maybe eight feet
... a long, hopeless wall of pounding hurricane waves.
I watched Doobs drop to the bottom and try for a turn
only to stall dead in the water and then have another
foamhead drop straight down out of the sky on his
back.

That was when I discovered that I really liked
seeing other guys get wasted ... even if they were
people I called my friends. I figured that everybody
had been dumping on me for long enough. I might as
well get my jollies watching other guys get whipped
around in this meat market.

I saw a few foamheads struggle into the beach,
having lost a fin or two. Total defeat. That made me

smile. I paddled further outside and paddled for big green rolling swell. I cranked my board hard high up on the wave ... no time for a bottom turn ... then I began to drive it fully-juiced on down the line. I could see a couple of foamheads about to drop in, not paying a bit of attention to me. I kicked out rather than smash into them at ninety miles an hour and scramble their brains.

But when I went for another wave, setting myself up just perfect again, high on the long green wall, I saw the same thing about to happen. I screamed at the first guy, "My wave!" He turned his head, saw me aimed straight for him like a kamikaze pilot. There was sheer panic in his face. I was sucking it up. He pulled himself backwards, giving me just enough room to squeeze through, then he got sucked over and down the front of the wave like he had just washed down Niagara Falls.

When I saw another young foamhead about to drop in on me, I was getting really annoyed. This was my ocean after all. I had surfed this place longer than anyone and I didn't like this business of young punks wrecking my rides. So I kicked high up into the face of water, right where the intruder was about to drop. As I sliced straight up at the kid, I cut back hard and grabbed onto his board, yanking it out from under him and throwing it up in the air. That took care of him.

The only problem was that it took care of me too. I was headed into this bowl section where the wave was now breaking in front of me. I was off-balance from dumping the little squirt and I should have kicked out if I had been in control. Instead, I found myself driving straight into a very hollow, very nasty overhead tube that was cracking down right on the inside sandbar.

Now, I never trusted beachbreak. That's where people get messed up, because you sometimes have nothing to come down on but sand and rock. I preferred water. For a split second, it was all very exciting. I mean, I had just aimed myself like a bullet straight into the throat of a killer tube. I heard an ear-splitting roar and watched this fantastic light show of sunlight pouring into this green room. But then came something just short of an earthquake. One second I was upright, the next thing I knew my feet were still on my board but it was above my head and I was hanging upside down inside the tube. Mind you, this all happened pretty quick.

I took a big gulp of air and waited for the worst. I didn't have to wait long. It was like the fist of a giant had picked me up and slammed me down hard on the sand in an explosion of whitewater. The white water began to boil now and I felt my arms and legs get pulled in different directions. The beach was steep here and I felt myself being driven up along gritty pebbles that scraped at my face and hands. I tried to pop up for air but the angry fist kept holding me down. The waves washed me right up to the sea wall and when I could finally get my head up, I saw people on the beach scrambling for the rocks as the shorebreak washed up over their blankets and towels.

Shaking my head to get the confusion out, I felt myself being dragged back down the sand in the backwash until another wave slammed me again. That was when I noticed that the first wave had snapped my leash. Somewhere in this mess, my new board was bashing around. I stood up and tried to stay upright when the next pounder hit. I saw the board all the way up by the rocks, wedged in between two big jagged boulders. Damn. As the beach crowd scrambled to get away from the shorebreak, I hung tough through the backwash and then ran for my board. The leash had been snapped clean in half. There was a big gash from where it had smashed into the seawall.

I was really mad. I looked back out to sea for the kid who had tried to drop in on me and made me mess up on the wave. I could see a few foamheads struggling to get out of the same shorebreak that had just knocked me around. I wanted to go lay into them but just then I saw this lifeguard running up to me.

This guy was blowing real loud on a stupid whistle like he was a football coach or something. He kept yelling, "Hey, you!" at me until he jogged up to within inches of my face.

He had on a bright yellow sweatshirt and a floater on his back. His nose was orange zinc oxide and the guy looked very tanned like he'd been hanging out in a tanning salon. (Lord knows we hadn't had enough sun lately for anyone to get that tan on the beach.)

He stuck his big fat face right up to me and said, "You know you could have really hurt somebody with that board. All these people swimming here had to get the heck out of your way. You could have really done some damage. If you can't control your board, bozo, then you shouldn't be in the ocean. Now stay away from where people are swimming."

I looked around and saw that everyone was watching. I wanted to say something back but my vocal chords were frozen in my throat. Who were all these people on the beach, anyway? What were they doing here, in my town? And what right did that jerk have to lecture me?

My board needed immediate attention and I needed a new surf leash. People looked at me like I had just committed a crime. A little skinny kid not more than thirteen came over. His head was scraped up and he had blood dripping down his face. "I shouldn't have tried to drop in on you," he said.

But I wasn't up for small talk or being polite. "Buzz off, kid. Just be more careful next time."

When I walked over the rocks, I saw Cathy there waiting for me. She didn't say anything; she just gave me a wicked look that made me feel about three inches tall. Driving home, I had a hard time seeing where I was going. I realized that I was about to start crying and I had no idea why.

Chapter Seventeen

Serious Surfing

I glassed my board back into shape in my old man's shop and put on my spare leash. Two days went by and I did nothing but surf. I'd get up early in the morning and find my own private waves before the townies even showed up. The water stayed warm, the waves stayed big and I was in better shape than I'd ever been. Surfing was wearing off the flab. And since I didn't have to wear a wetsuit all the time, I was starting to look tanned. The hurricane was still off-shore and was tracking in a lazy zig-zag pattern that just kept pumping waves at us.

It was like the whole province had suddenly remembered we had an ocean. By noon, Lawrencetown looked like Coney Island with cars jammed everywhere. The beach was bumper to bumper oiled bodies and sometimes, in the afternoons, I'd just walk around gawking at the ladies in two-piece bathing suits. The whole scene was unreal.

It had only been a few days since Kevin had been at sea but I had long since forgotten about work. All I wanted to do was surf and I wasn't about to let all the townies get waves that I rightfully deserved.

So when Kevin woke me up on Thursday and said that he was ready to go out to sea again, I said, "No way."

"C'mon Rankle. We're losing money, man. Gulf Minot went out yesterday and he says he got enough hake to fill the whole boat. Something to do with the hurricane bringing in fish from the Banks. Let's go."

I was groggy and still half asleep. All I knew was that the last thing in the world I wanted to do right then was go out on my brother's fishing boat.

"Forget the fish. Forget the money," I told him. "It's not worth it. It's just too dangerous." I had seen the satellite pictures. This was one motherlode of a hurricane that had not diminished. It had doubled back from Newfoundland and was sitting just east of of Sable Island. I had never heard of a tropical storm doing that. The weather office had predicted that the seas would actually get bigger before getting smaller.

"Then I'll just have to go myself," Kev said.

I took a deep breath. My brother could be pretty stubborn sometimes. It ran in our family. I lay back for a second, trying to muster some energy to wake up and go explain to him about the satellite photographs, the weather report. But I guess I goofed because I fell back asleep.

When I woke up, I thought only a couple of minutes had passed but I looked at the clock and it said 9:30.

I threw on my pants and stumbled into the kitchen where my mother was bottling pickled herring.

"Where'd Kevin go?"

"He went fishing," she said. "He was getting too rammy hanging around the house, I think." She didn't seem worried about the storm at sea.

"How come you didn't go with him?" she asked.

"Aw, I wanted to go surfing. He's been fishing without me before." Mom didn't seem too concerned. "Kevin knows what he's doing, I guess. He always does," she said.

She was wrong, though. I knew better. Kevin didn't always know what he was doing. If he did, he wouldn't have taken the boat out. I hoped that he'd have another scare in the inlet and give it up. Just to be sure, though, I drove the Caddie out to Causeway Road and looked around. No sign of Kevin or his boat.

He and a couple of the others had taken their boats out early, Giff DeLong told me. I looked at the swell in the inlet. It didn't look that bad. But way out past Rat Rock I could see what looked like clouds ... only they weren't clouds, they were heavy ground swells breaking on the reefs far out where usually no waves broke.

Giff saw what I was staring at. "Don't worry, lad. As long as he steers clear of them reefs, he should be okay in the deep water."

He was probably right. What was I going to do, hang around the wharf and worry over my big brother all day? Shoot, I had some serious surfing to do.

Chapter Eighteen

A Legend is Born

When I got to the beach, the waves were breathtaking. The lifeguards were keeping swimmers out of the water and for good reason. The shorebreak that had gobbled me up the other day was now even bigger. All the foamheads were just standing around the shore in awe of the waves. There were a dozen boards propped up around the beach. So it had finally come to this.

Out to sea, I could make out maybe three fishing boats with stern sails. Out there it was probably just a lot of up and down heaving ... but as long as they stayed out there, I could see that it might not be so bad. The wind was light. The chop was minimal.

I guessed the wave off the point was maybe twelve feet high, by far the biggest I'd ever seen it break. But was it rideable? There was no easy place to paddle through to get outside without having to dive under or punch through massive walls of water. But if somebody could get out there, what a rush it would be to drop in on one of these monsters.

I watched as two of the new townies tried paddling out from the headland only to get washed far down the beach and gobbled by the shorebreak. It was still kind of fun to see the new guys get trounced. But after I saw Reggie and Chris fail in their attempt to make it outside, I began to wonder if anybody could. Was it worth it?

It looked like no one was going to get any waves. It was just too massive, too out of control. Hundreds of people were lined up along the rocks, just watching the sea. I'd never seen people so hooked on just watching waves. But the crowd scene was a little too weird for me. I decided I'd go home. I didn't need to get pounded. I'd wait for the swell to ease up.

That's when I saw Brian, Fitz and Belcher scrambling off the rocks. They had waited for a break in the sets and finally found it. All three were paddling as if their lives depended on it. Some people on the rocks cheered them on.

Fitz and Brian scrambled over the top of two waves just before they collapsed into a swirling nightmare of thundering soup. Belcher wasn't so lucky. The lip caught him and threw him down the face of the wave. He hit and I saw him dive deep. The kid had learned a few things, I guess. As Fitz and Brian kept paddling to get out beyond the break, I watched Belcher lose his board and get washed way down the beach. The lifeguards kept an eye on him but didn't go after him. He was okay. Besides, it would have been impossible for the lifeguards with their long paddle boards to push out through the tons of whitewater ploughing towards shore.To tell you the truth, watching Belcher, I would have been happy to just go home. But there were Brian and Fitz, sitting on their boards, probably scared out of their wits, but they had made it outside. And now, here was Cathy walking over to me. She looked worried.

"They shouldn't be out there, should they?" Cathy asked. She was really thinking about Brian.

"Probably not. But hey, Brian can handle himself."

Then, as a big wall of water thundered over very close to shore and threw spray two stories up in the air, she shuddered. Cathy was really scared. It was that sudden shaking of her shoulders that made me realize that she really did love Brian. I should have known that all along. "I blew it , didn't I?" I said.

"What do you mean?"

"We could have been good friends."

"Yeah, we could have." But I could see that she didn't understand what I was just figuring out.

"You going out?"

"Yeah, why not?" I played it very loose. I didn't want to go in right then. Cathy's fear had rubbed off. I wanted to see Brian and Fitz get washed back into shore and that would be that.

Instead, I watched as Brian paddled for a looming peak and, with his arms swept back from the take-off, he dropped down the face of a ten-footer. When he was out on the flat at the bottom, he got himself too far in front of the wave, lost his speed and couldn't turn. He dove off his board just as the freight train wave rumbled by. His cord held and he popped right back up and paddled back for the line-up. Fitz was just sitting way out there. I could tell that he wasn't too anxious to do the same.

"I'd feel better if you were out there with Brian," she said.

"He can handle himself," I lied. "But no sweat, I'll go out to catch a few rides, anyway."

Cathy lit up in a smile and gave me a hug. People were watching and I know that I turned a bright red just then.

"I counted twenty-five waves in the last set before a single break," Cathy told me, "but it only lasted less than a minute. I've never seen anything quite like it."

"Me neither," I admitted. All the way walking out to the point, I reminded myself that the water was warm ... it was nothing like those days at the Big Left. All that could happen would be that you'd get rolled by a wave and washed in.

I couldn't find a hole between sets so I just had to bully my way out. It took me twenty minutes and I was plain beat by the time I paddled over to Fitz and Brian.

"Cathy sends her regards," I said to Brian.

Brian shook his head. "All I'd like right now is a nice five-foot wave and an easy ride straight in," he admitted. This wasn't like the old Brian at all.

"Yeah, me too," said Fitz.

"I thought you dudes came out here for a little action," I said, my eyes fixed on a double-overhead cruncher that was rolling by just a few yards away. I watched it slam over and spit spray out of the green room hard enough to knock a man off his feet.

"After you?" Brian said.

I figured I didn't have much choice. I waited for a set, let five waves roll by and began to paddle for the sixth. The slight offshore breeze kicked up into a full force gale by the time I got moving and the bottom of the sea had been pulled out from under me.

My right foot was on the tail as I flew to the bottom of the wave and leaned, ever so gently, afraid to lose my necessary speed. There, the turn was done. I was moving back high up on the wall, the top of the wave towering above me. I was racing so fast that my board was starting to bounce off the chop on the face of the wave. If I wasn't careful I was going to lose it. But I hunkered down. For once, I felt glad that I had weight. It helped keep me stone steady.

I looked way down the line and could see a quarter mile section of wave about to pitch over. There was no way I was going to make it. So I drove hard straight up the face of the wave and catapulted into space. What a feeling! It was like absolute freedom. As the wave passed, I was maybe ten feet up in the sky and spread eagled. I splashed down, my board right alongside of me in calm water. I was in the deep and it was an easy paddle back to the line-up. I could hear cheers from the beach and car horns blasting. A legend had been born.

Brian looked more nervous than ever. "Luck, man. That was very lucky," he said.

"Skill, buddy. I like to think of it as skill."

And to prove my point, I did it again. And a third time. Each time, I was a little more radical. I carved hard off the lip, I lay back closer into the curl, I raced faster down the wall and kicked out later and closer to the close out.

The wind up the face of the waves was getting stronger. Brian and Fitz were having a hard time taking off; they were getting blown off the back.

Finally Brian connected with dumpy seven-footer that allowed him a bit of a ride. He paddled back out and caught another one like it.

Fitz had grown reckless after seeing me thrash and he went for a wave way too big and way too late. I've still got this image in my head from up close of seeing the guy all tangled up with his board, falling down the face of the twelve-foot wave, bouncing off, halfway down and then getting shot up into the air as the entire Atlantic Ocean came hammering down on him like a nuclear bomb.

I saw some of the other guys run out to the point and fish him and his board off the rocks. After he got his breath, it looked like he could walk so I figured he was okay.

The scene made Brian pretty nervous again. "I'm headed in," he said. "Wish me luck."

He picked off a ten-foot green wall that gave him a very smooth take-off and room to spare before it went critical. He didn't make any fancy moves, but he did make it a long way down towards the sandbar break. What he forgot to do was kick out before the bowl and the crunch. He saw it coming too late, tried to kick his board away but went down hanging onto it ... not a very smart move.

To tell you the truth, I *had* been lucky. I'd picked just the right waves and made perfectly timed take-offs. I had been smart and got out before the mangling but I admit, it was luck, too. That's why I decided I didn't want to sit out in the Atlantic Ocean all by myself. I knew the longer I sat there, the more nervous I'd get.

I grabbed the first wave that came along. As I took off, I knew I was on the late side. I saw the thing scoop out over top of my brains and begin to heave itself forward. I had to crouch down and grab a rail to force a turn high up on the face. That put me into a semi-controlled slide, but the whole thing was way too steep. One of my fins popped out and I realized I was slipping sideways down the front of the wave. It was going to be a sucker trap for sure.

I stood up, slipped my foot back for a bit more tail control and carved a wonderfully stupid turn of desperation. I was hoping to simply shoot out front on the flat and belly ride my board in. But what I did was accidentally jam a turn that threw me way back into the tube and the break of the wave. All at once I was at the top and connecting with the lip. I was nearly upside down but I dug in the tail hard. Where the hell was I going anyway? I had jabbed a nearly midair turn and was now coming over with the full force of the exploding wave. I kept wanting to believe I was in control but I knew that it was all an accident.

Then suddenly I was off the lip and fading down over the white water. I wouldn't find my way back onto the clean wall of the wave, but I had just executed the most amazing in-the-air kickback of my lifetime. The whitewater was driving me straight into the rocks at the foot of the headland and I let myself go until I had to jump off, and act as an anchor to keep my board (and me) from getting bashed. I toughed out some nasty soup, then scrambled up on the rocks and halfway up the headland face to get out of the way of the next incoming set.

Down on the beach, I saw that Brian and Fitz were walking back to the rocks. Cathy was with them. We had all had enough surfing for one day.

Chapter Nineteen

Drifting Toward Shore

As I walked up to the road, I really liked the way people looked at me. They either thought I was crazy or they thought I had a lot of guts to be out there surfing those monsters. I sucked in my stomach and felt like I was two feet taller than I actually was.

But the glow didn't last long. The road was all jammed up with traffic. People had parked their cars half on the road and now there was a bottleneck with cars coming from either way, fighting each other to get through. It was looking like a real circus. I saw the two parks planners walking around taking pictures that they could use as evidence later to chase us out of this end of the beach.

"Hey," I said to them, "these aren't surfers. You can't blame us for this." And I looked around just to make sure. Every car that belonged to a surf townie or a foamhead was off the road, parked legally.

I realized I'd never get my Caddie out of this mess, so I figured I might as well settle in with the gawkers and watch the ocean. I thought maybe I could get some mileage out of my wave riding to meet a new lady. I knew I might as well give up on Cathy. She was down there on the beach lying down on a blanket with

Brian who was still recovering from his session in the water. It made me want to cry just looking at her.

I saw the traffic up the hill open up to let a Mountie through. I knew it would be Darlene and I swore that I'd treat her like gold.

Darlene pulled to a stop and got on her loudspeaker, telling everyone to move their cars.

"Hi, cousin," I said to her, not caring who saw me this time.

She put down the microphone. "Hi, Randy. I hope you're not parked on the road 'cause I'm gonna start handing out tickets." She sounded really rattled and she was sweating.

"No, I'm okay. Do your duty." I said. "Let me know if I can help." But I was only joking.

Then I noticed that people were pointing out to sea. I squinted my eyes hard against the sun and looked, expecting to see some other poor slob of a surfer trying to get out through the waves but there were none to be seen.

Then a shudder went through me like the biggest, most gnarly wave of all time had just slammed me down onto the stony beach. A fishing boat was maybe half a mile offshore. He seemed way too close in for the kind of ocean we had today.

Darlene was writing out her first ticket. "You have binoculars with you?" I asked.

"Sure, on the front seat," she said. "What is it?"

I ran to her car and took them out. As soon as I got the boat in focus, I felt all the blood in my body drain down to my toes. It was Kevin. And he was standing over the engine, waving his arms and cursing at it from the looks of things. That told me the whole deadly story.

Darlene had followed me. She understood even before I said anything. "Kevin?"

"Yeah. He's in trouble."

Darlene got on the radio immediately and radioed the Lawrencetown Fire House for the rescue crew.

"They've got a zodiac," she told me. "They'll be here in twenty minutes."

"Damn." I said, slamming my fist down hard on top of the police car. "He wouldn't listen to me."

"Don't think about that now," Darlene said.

I looked hard again through the binocs. Kevin had gone inside. "Darlene, can you get Marine Band on that?"

She punched a button and the radio began to automatically scan. There it was.

"Come in. Anybody out there? Hey look, if you can hear me, I'm in a boat just off Lawrencetown Beach. No power. I'm drifting in toward shore. I need help. Come in!"

I grabbed the mike. "Kev, buddy, it's me. I'm on the beach. Darlene's here. She called the rescue squad. What's up?"

"I took a wave over the side. Water in the engine. Right down the old carb. I tried draining it but no luck."

"Did you check all the wires and spray everything dry?"

"Yeah. I tried everything. I'm screwed, Randy."

"Hang tight. A zodiac's coming."

Darlene started shouting at people to get their cars out of the way. "This is an emergency," she said. "We gotta get a rescue truck in here. Now everybody, get in your cars and move it. Now!"

People responded slowly and I felt like walking around punching some turkeys in the face. I paced around nervously, keeping an eye on the boat. He wasn't there yet, but slowly and surely, Kevin was headed straight into the monster waves cracking far out off the beach. I picked up the mike. "How's she going, Kev? We got everything under control here," I lied.

"Not good, Rankle. It don't look one bit good. I tried to rig the sail to help pull me out to sea. I think it's slowing me down but I'm still headed in. What'll I do, man?"

"Just hang tight. We'll get you." I threw down the microphone. Darlene tried to put her arm around my shoulder. "He'll be okay," she said.

But I didn't see any sign of the rescue truck. Twenty minutes was too long to do nothing. I'd had enough waiting. As I pulled away, Darlene grabbed at my arm but I shook it off. "No, Randy," she said. But I was already running.

I grabbed my board and scrambled over the rocks, running past Brian, who had his arm around Cathy. They didn't know what was going on. "Man, you got to be crazy to go back out there," Brian yelled to me. "It's friggin' insane out there."

Cathy broke away from Brian and ran towards me. She grabbed my arm and nearly wrenched it off. The girl was much stronger than I expected. I could see that she didn't want me to go out. I could see that she cared. "Do you know what you're doing?" she asked.

"No," I answered, "I don't, but thanks for asking."

I didn't wait for a break in the waves. I just ran straight out through the shallows, heaved my board down and paddled like hell. I punched through four big walls of water and then got on my knees and paddled hard. A current had me and I was moving down the beach. I knew I was in the absolutely wrong place. I was headed down towards where Kevin was but I was a long way away yet. Adrenalin was pumping. I was determined to push through however many waves I had to to get to Kevin. I didn't even want to think about what good it would do if I got there.

I was losing ground fast, though. I could punch through two waves if I really struggled but, before I could get my breath, a third wave would dump me and pound the living daylights out of me. I would get back up on my board and paddle, but the same thing would happen again. After about twelve poundings, I got the wind fully knocked out of me and couldn't breathe.

That's when I felt pure, cold panic set in. Still not able to breathe, I dove deep to save my strength and when I came up, I realized I had lost any chance of getting out. There was nothing but close-out sets that broke top-to-bottom all at once down the entire length of the beach. The next wave washed me up on shore, where I landed hard, spread-eagled and clawing at the stones, just to keep from getting washed back out.

When I could finally stand up and pick up my board, I felt like I was going to puke. I was dizzy from lack of oxygen and my head was swimming. But I hadn't given up. I ran back down the beach, all the while looking at the sea for an opening, some place where I could get out through the waves. All I could see were piles of whitewater and raging faces of waves. I wouldn't give up.

When I made it back to the headland I tried again. But I wasn't more than ten feet off shore when the whole horrible rerun began. I was weaker now too, but I prayed that I'd be able to luck-out and paddle through.

As I was fighting with waves, I saw behind me that the zodiac had arrived. Six men in survival suits had the rubber boat on the beach and were trying to get it started. At least I had allies, I figured.

But I was getting nowhere. The current had pulled me way down the beach again and all I could do was groan and dive deep when wave after wave pounded over my head. I figured that pretty soon, one of these monsters would snap my leash and then I'd be really screwed. I couldn't see Kevin's boat from here and had completely lost my bearings as I bobbed up and down between huge troughs of water and swirling masses of soup. Finally, my arms just seemed to stop working and I let myself drift back into shore where I crawled up out of the water.

I half-ran, half-stumbled back down the beach. The zodiac was off. Fantastic. The men had got it started and they were pushing away from shore.

I climbed up on the rocks to look for Kevin's boat. There he was. Less than a quarter mile out now. You could see him standing on the deck waving his arms. I squinted hard, wanting to see orange. I wanted to see that he had on a lifejacket. I couldn't tell for sure, but it didn't look like it.

Then I realized I didn't even have to guess. I was the one who always picked up the lifejackets and threw them on the boat. One of Kevin's screwy fears was that people would steal stuff laying around the boat. So we kept all the gear locked up in the shed. And I was the one who always grabbed the lifegear. Kevin wouldn't have it on, the idiot.

Chapter Twenty

Down the Face of a Wave

A s soon as I saw the zodiac take the first wave head
on and stand itself straight up in the air, I knew
they didn't stand a chance. The men were volunteers
— three gutsy local heroes who were willing to go out
in the raging sea to try and save my brother. But this
was all new to them. We almost never had waves this
big and they had never been foolish enough to prac-
tice in an ocean this mean.

I watched as they hung onto the ropes to keep from
falling out. They tried bravely to conquer the next two
waves but each time, the best they could do was to
keep from losing ground. The next wave broke further
out and the whitewater slammed into the zodiac,
knocking two men off. They took a heavy pounding
from the sea, then bobbed back up in their bright red
survival suits. One guy washed back in and the other
two made it back into the boat. By now they had
drifted into the same trap that I had been in. They
were too close to the sand bar and wave after angry
hollow wave slammed down on them. There was no
way they could drive up over the face of any of them
and the sea was not giving anybody a break. They
turned back to shore as a spectacular, vicious

shorebreak grabbed the boat and pitched it over, spilling the men on the shallows near the beach. People watching along the shore ran down to help them out of the water.

There were no sets, no breaks between sets, just wave after bloody wave. And there was my poor, scared-to-death brother almost to the line of the outside breaker. I had never felt more helpless in my life. I closed my eyes and clenched my fists and tried to fight back the tears.

That's when somebody grabbed me hard from behind. I opened my eyes. Brian. "Look, man," he said. He pointed toward the headland. I almost didn't see it at first.

A rip had opened up along the shoreline and it snaked its way out toward the point. All that angry pounding shorebreak had opened up a sort of channel along the beach and now the water was spilling back out to sea, making its own river through the snarly waves.

"That's it," I said. And I ran like the wind. Somebody had given me back my lungs. And my arms. And my courage.

And as I threw my board down in the water and hopped on, I realized that I wasn't alone. Brian was right there beside me. "Paddle like hell, dude," he said. And we paddled.

Brian had been right. In seconds we were caught up in the rip and headed straight out to sea. Big bulging swells just passed under us as we paddled until we were all the way out in deep water, near the point.

Now we had to turn and paddle parallel to the coast if we wanted to get to Kevin. I kept wanting to say something to Brian but I was breathing so hard that I couldn't get the words out. Finally I had to speak. "Why are you doing this?" I asked.

"You saved my butt once, remember. The Big Left. If it wasn't for you, I would have been mincemeat. Now shut up and paddle."

I had never paddled so long and so hard. Kevin saw us and kept waving. It was probably only ten minutes but it seemed like forever. *What's the plan?* I kept asking myself. *What are we going to do, once we get there?* Maybe Brian had an idea. He was a smart guy and he had more guts than anyone I ever met. Maybe he'd know what to do. I tried not to think about it.

Water was lapping up over the sides of the boat when we got to her. We climbed up and hauled our boards in.

Kevin was walking around the deck in ankle deep water muttering, "Now what are we going to do?" over and over.

As each new swell lifted the boat, you could see high over the dunes and all the way up Lawrencetown Lake. I grabbed the wheel and got us pointed straight out to sea. At least we wouldn't get swamped by being sideways. Brian and Kev tried to tighten the jib so that it might catch a bit more of the offshore wind and pull us out but it didn't do any good. A wave crashed over just yards shoreward from where the boat was. That was it. Plan B was in order.

"Get him on your board, Randy," Brian ordered. "We'll take our time and stay out here in deep water and go in the way we came out."

I wanted to tell Brian it wouldn't work. Even if we could make it back to the rip, we wouldn't be able to paddle against it to get in. And there'd be no way I could surf my board with Kevin on it without getting wasted. Kevin couldn't swim. He'd never make it.

But the clock had run out. There was no more time to decide what to do. A twelve-foot wave smashed over the bow and sent a shiver down the length of the boat. It snapped the jib off and the mast as well.

"Brian, get out of here," I said. "You don't have to hang around for this." He could see what I was getting at. He picked up his board and tied the leash around his ankle. He was about to jump over the side when he suddenly stopped.

"No, I think I'm along for the entire cruise. Why leave you guys here to have all the fun?" I don't know where he got up the nerve to come up with that line but it cracked right through my haze of panic. I knew that it was up to me to save Kevin, but now I felt like I had somebody on my side.

"All right, Clem, let's see what we can do," I said. I cranked hard on the wheel. Without any power, it was slow, dangerous turnaround. I held my breath as we were perfectly sideways to a wave that just barely allowed us over the top.

And then I had the bow aimed perfectly straight for shore. If I could just keep the rudder steady. Maybe.

Maybe it's just as well that I didn't have any more time to think through just how foolish and stupid this manoeuvre was going to be.

A wave was beginning to break behind us. We started to slide down the face of it but it broke hard top to bottom so that we took the full brunt of it. Water like cannon fire hammered down on all of us and filled the deck.

Brian had his arm wrapped up in a rope tied to the hull and he reached out with his other arm and grabbed Kevin as he was about to get swept over the side.

I was still hanging onto the steering wheel. I wasn't even sure now which way I had the rudder. We were still pointed towards shore but we were a long way out. Another wave like that and the boat would be in splinters.

"Hang on!" I yelled as I saw another, even bigger wave form behind us. I saw the top begin to come over and expected the worst. I was afraid to keep staring at the wave, so I watched the deck as it tilted up on a forty-five degree angle and water began to spill out. My brother was scrambling to get on his feet and couldn't, but Brian was hanging on to him.

We had been surrounded by the roar of thundering waves like we were in the middle of a war but then suddenly I felt the wind in my face and there was a split second of silence.

We were dropping down the face of a wave, possibly fifteen feet high. I could see up over the dunes again. I saw the green of the spruce trees on the hillsides above the lake. Time seemed to have come to a stop.

The drop went on forever. Then we were at the bottom. We had gained enough speed on the descent to scoot us out yards in front of the wave and then it came over like an avalanche behind us. By the time the whitewater reached us, still boiling in a six-foot mass of death, it washed over the stern but kept pushing us shoreward.

I was still hanging onto the wheel when the bow was driven like a sharp nail into the loose stones and sand of the beach. I let go and grabbed for Kevin and Brian. "Let's get out of here!"

We jumped over the side and struggled through the backwash as we saw the boat begin to slip back toward the sea.

Now that the boat was sideways, the next wave flipped her over completely and jackhammered down on it. We were all laying in the sand, gasping when people began gathering around us.

"I've got this funny feeling that we're still alive," Brian said, pushing away one of the rescue workers who was asking him if he was okay.

Chapter Twenty-one

From Here On ...

Two days later the sea calmed down and it was like nothing had ever happened. Foamheads and townies were out surfing three-foot mush and loving it. I had finally figured out how to just lie around on the beach and do nothing. I was working hard at being lazy and discovered that it was a skill I was born for. I started talking to everyone and couldn't believe how friendly people were if I gave them half a chance.

For some reason, Brian and Cathy disappeared from the scene. I asked Fitz what was going on and he told me that Brian got a job working as a bellhop at the Sheraton Hotel because he was broke. He'd spent all his allowance money on surf gear and his old man finally told him he had to pay his own bills. I almost felt bad for the guy. I wondered how this would affect his relationship with Cathy. In fact, I have to admit that I wondered if I might have some time to spend with Cathy now that Brian was tied up working. I still had a thing for the girl and wondered if this might be my lucky break.

Unfortunately, it turned out that she took a job too. She was now a waitress at a fancy restaurant. I tried calling her house a couple of times but she was never in and I was too chicken to leave a message with her mother.

Then one night, when I was sitting around playing rummy with my father and Kev, I saw Brian's hot little car pull up outside. He and Cathy got out and I thought, this is going to be a really bizarre scene. What are they going to think of my house and my family? It's going to be a nightmare.

Instead, Brian greeted Kev at the door like he was a long lost buddy. My father just sort of cleaned up the cards, tipped his hat to the lady and grabbed the newspaper, retreating to a seat in front of the T.V. where my mother was watching a rerun of Dallas.

"How have the waves been, dude?" Brian asked.

"Whipped," I answered. "Not a thing worth getting your big toe wet for." Having mentioned big toes, I suddenly remember the photo I had taken of Cathy's. I looked at her and she gave me a knowing, cute little smile.

"That's good news," Brian said, not clueing in on the joke. "I can't stand the thought of being in town working while you're out here getting tubed." But he didn't mean it in a nasty way. He punched me on the shoulder like he was playing tag. I smiled at the guy and decided again that I really did like him. He was all right. To make himself more at home, he took off his yellow windbreaker and handed it to Cathy like she was his servant. Cathy threw it on the floor but Brian didn't notice. She looked at me, and spinning her finger around her ear, she pointed to Brian, meaning the guy was really flaked; he still hadn't caught on to a few things yet.

My old dog, Diefenbaker, walked into the room, saw the windbreaker on the floor, circled once and settled down on it for a snooze. Brian looked down just then at his spanking new jacket, gave Dief a look of disgust but he didn't say anything.

"What brings you out here, anyway?" I asked Cathy, figuring there must be some reason they came. Brian looked around at every corner of the kitchen, craned his neck to see my old man and my mom watching TV in the next room. You could tell it was all new to him.

"I heard back from the deputy minister about the parking at the beach," she said.

"And you got nowhere, right?" I asked, expecting the worst.

"Well, not exactly," she answered. "He told me that thanks to the TV coverage of surfers rescuing a fisherman at the beach, it's not going to be easy to write you guys off."

Kevin was listening. You could tell he still didn't like the idea of "having to be rescued." I think it hurt his ego a bit. But as he mulled it over, he saw a new angle in it. "Hey, that's why I staged the whole thing. I was just trying to help you guys out." But he was just goofing. Cathy and Brian laughed. Kevin gave me a wink and faded from the kitchen. When he was out of Cathy's vision, Kevin looked at her and then at me, shook his hand in the air the way he does when he sees a pretty girl, meaning he thought she was pretty hot looking. I waved my hand at him to get him out of the room before he said something really stupid.

Cathy added, "In fact, that's why we came out tonight. After I talked to the deputy minister, I talked to the parks officials. They still think surfers are a bunch of reckless jerks. They said it doesn't matter what the surfers want, they're going to go through with their plan."

"It sucks," Brian said. "Maybe we should try sab-otage."

Cathy smacked him on the head with the flat of her hand. "Shut up a minute," she told him, " I'm not done. The deputy minister said that we can save the place if we put pressure on the politicians. So we're trying to get everyone who cares to call up their MLA and protest. They shouldn't have the right to make the beach so inaccessible."

"Do you think it will work?" I asked.

"Yeah," she said. "I think it will. I've already talked to lots of kids. Even the foamheads said they were willing to get involved."

I stuck a militant fist in the air and shouted "Liberate Lawrencetown Beach!"

Brian looked at me like I was a bit of a loonie tune so I sat back down at the table. He was so used to being the centre of everything that he tried to steer the conversation back to himself. "This working thing is really weird," he said. "Like I got all these really up-tight dudes telling me what to do all the time. And I gotta carry these suitcases for some wimped-out turkeys who should have to carry their own stuff. I think I'd rather do what your brother does."

"Fish?" I asked him in total disbelief.

"Yeah. I like the idea of being out to sea in a boat. You could, like, check the waves and stuff."

"Right," I snapped back. "Stuff like tear up your hands on fish line and walk around up to your armpits in fish guts and slime."

"Sounds better than trying to be polite to the slime buckets I gotta cater to."

"You have my sympathy," I told him sarcastically.

I guess Brian was feeling a little sorry for himself. "Now that my father's on this pay-your-own-way kick, he says he might not pay my tuition to McGill when I graduate."

I was trying to remember what the heck McGill was and then it clicked that it was a university in Montreal. "But I told my old man," Brian continued, "I didn't want to go to McGill, it was too far from the ocean. I said I'd go to Saint Mary's or Dalhousie and I'd take out a loan or something."

"What about you?" Cathy asked, trying to get me back into the conversation.

"School, you mean?"

"Yeah, what are you going to do when you graduate?"

I almost didn't know what to say. In fact, I had been thinking about the possibility of not going back to school in the fall at all, of just working with Kevin if we could figure out a way to get another boat in the water. But I looked at her and I realized I couldn't tell her I might quit. I looked at Cathy, still realizing I didn't have a snowball's chance in hell with her, but began to wonder how the heck I was going to meet any other girl like her if I didn't maybe hang around school for a few more years. I was sure as hell not going to meet any women two miles out to sea hand-lining for cod.

"I don't know," I told her. "I'll be lucky if I make it through high school. Then I'll have to see what happens."

"You'll make it, " she told me.

Right then I realized that even if she's not going to ever be my girlfriend, Cathy and I are going to be friends for a long time to come.

I fixed up the Cadillac some more and sold it to one of the foamheads from Halifax who had just turned sixteen. He gave me five hundred bucks for it, admitting it was his parents' money. I put the cash and all the rest I had saved towards another boat. Kevin had some insurance but not enough. But when we pooled our money we had enough to buy a used boat, almost as good as new. Now we'd be partners. I'd work in the summers and on weekends and when I was in school, we'd pay the Bellefontaine boy to go out with Kevin. Kevin also finally promised me that he would learn to swim.

I painted my old Chevette with some leftover baby- blue paint that my old man had in his shop and it didn't look half bad. I liked driving a car that didn't gobble so much gas.

Darlene and I went to play bingo a couple of nights last week and it was almost like the old days. She said she was still having a hard time fitting in back home now that she was a Mountie. And I had always had a hard time fitting in anywhere, so I figured we had a lot in common.

She was off duty one day and just hanging out at the beach with me when those two creepy parks people came by. Summer was over and the crowds had split. We could see by the way they were talking that they were making plans to put in the guard rails again and close down the surf spot for good now that there weren't a bunch of townies around to give the workmen a hard time.

"When do you plan on doing the work?" Darlene asked. They didn't recognize her without her uniform.

"We'll have this place closed off by the middle of next week."

"That's not fair," I said. I looked down to the official parking lot that already had a chain across it. It looked like it was closed for the winter.

Darlene shook her head and told me to be quiet.

"Have you considered that you might be breaking federal and provincial beach access laws by that action?"

"Look, we work for the province. This is a park and our job is to develop this place for the use of all people."

"Precisely," Darlene said and she began to run off a whole string of numbers ... bill this and bill that ... that she thought they might be breaking if they tried to limit the use of a beach that had been free and open to people in Lawrencetown for generations.

After they were flabbergasted and gone, Darlene told me, "From here on, this is your battle, buster. I'll give you all the information you need but I can't get myself in the middle of it or my boss is going to scream."

"That's okay," and I knew that I was ready to fight for this place. No parks planners were going to keep me away from here. I'd toughed out worse situations than this. And, besides, I wasn't alone. I had friends, lots of them, and they wouldn't be afraid to help me out. Maybe it would even be fun.

Glossary

beachbreak (or shorebreak) — waves that break close to the shoreline with considerable force as the wave spends itself in shallow water.

boogie board — a short board made of soft foam, sometimes with a rigid plastic bottom, surfed by riding on one's stomach or knees.

bottom turn — after the take-off, the first turn made at the bottom of the wave to set up for a ride *along* the face of the wave, instead of straight in to shore.

choppy — bumpy water due to local strong or gusty winds.

close-out — a wave or set of waves that break all at once, top-to-bottom over an extended area. Impossible to surf.

ding — an injury to the surfboard.

floater —a surfing move whereby the surfer kicks his board up over breaking whitewater and "floats" back down to the bottom of the wave creating an almost weightless sensation.

foamhead — a term, affectionately derogatory, for someone who rides a boogie board made of soft foam.

glassy — the smooth surface of the water if there are no local winds present.

goofy foot — someone who surfs with his right foot forward.

green room — that magical place, inside the tube of a hollow wave.

junk — lousy surf.

kick out — pushing down on the tail of the board to cut a complete 180 - degree turn, exiting the wave.

leash — a flexible cord attached to the surfer's ankle and tied to his board for easy retrieval after a wipe-out.

line up — the appropriate place to be sitting on your board, ready to catch a wave, as it approaches from sea.

over the falls — being driven over the face of the wave, top to bottom as the wave collapses, usually associated with being wiped-out.

overhead — a wave that is taller than the surfer, as in a *double overhead cruncher.*

rail — the edge of the surfboard; along with the fins used for turning and control.

rip (current) —a river of water moving parallel to shore or out to sea carrying back massive amounts of seawater brought shoreward by breaking waves.

roundhouse cutback — a long, sweeping arc made on the surfboard, often on the shoulder of the wave, whereby the surfer cuts back into the breaking section of a wave rather than away from it.

set — a group of waves.

stoked — excited.

swell — unbroken waves moving towards land, before they break in shallow water.

take-off — the start of the ride, requires strong paddling to match the speed of the wave.

thrashing — hot surfing.

tube — the hollow part of the wave created when the breaking top of the wave throws water out ahead making a sort of tunnel on the face of the wave. (To be *tubed*, then, is to be inside the hollow part while you're riding.)

wall — the face of the wave, usually before it is broken.

wipe-out — losing control and getting wasted by a wave.